A MAN OF HIS TIME

TERRY M DUNN

Terry M. Dunn

Published by Daneburyverse Books
Printed by Book Printing UK
Remus House, Coltsfoot drive,
Peterborough PE2 9BF
ISBN 978-1-9162657-2-1

For Teri, whose help in the production of this novel was much appreciated.

3,509 BC

1

All in all, things didn't seem to be going too badly.

At first.

The Chieftain of Danebury was satisfied. It was too much to expect him to be happy but he was quite satisfied with the way his village had made it through the winter.

Here in Neolithic southern England, 3500 years before the birth of Christ, the winters could be as cold and harsh as the summers were bright and hot and the people who lived off the land could quite easily find themselves at the mercy of the elements.

Only the Chieftain really knew the time in which he lived as the Neolithic or late Stone Age period. Knew this fact because he was a man out of time, his own time, shot back into the distant past by a terrible accident of technology during a military training exercise on Salisbury Plain in the year 1988.

All the other people who lived where he now lived were simple people of the time before history. Short, stocky of build and with simple values. They lived close to the land and close to the poverty line. But they loved life and lived it to the full. They worshipped their Goddess, honoured their village and their Chieftain, were people of their word, fought battles when necessary and, when the time came, invariably died well. Good people. People it made one proud to be associated with.

Although their general living conditions could be described as rough and the daily work hard, there was a natural harmony within the village, the surrounding lands and with Mother nature herself, a feeling of balance that flowed across the land. Yes, all in all things weren't going to badly and Parrish, the Chieftain of Danebury, was satisfied.

He stood looking out from the threshold of his log cabin, his usual vantage point where he regularly surveyed the village under his charge, looking out over the circular village huts that clustered together for protection behind the encompassing protective wall of Danebury hillfort. To his people who spoke a rather rudimentary early Gaelic/Celtic dialect, the name of their home was pronounced 'Dane-bre'. Theirs was one of several small, usually circular and singular communities dotted about the higher chalk ridges that made up the broad bands of high ground in Southern England called the downs. The people made occasional pilgrimages to the great temple of their Earth Goddess which was situated to the north of the territory, beyond the Marlborough Downs at Avebury, where a truly great circle of rough hewn stones marked the central hub of their religion. Other than that, the villages, who fought one another if the opportunity arose, kept much to themselves, generally only venturing out as regular hunting parties, or on some particular mission if a certain need arose, but these events were rare.

Parrish watched for a while as the people, his people, went about their business, be it to do with household chores, tending the flock of sheep away near the forests edge or working at the ground in the patchwork of as yet unseeded crop fields just beyond the confines and defensive ditch of Danebury hillfort. The fields were being made ready to receive the blessings of the holy man and the ritual planting of what would become the late summer crop of wheat.

Occasionally someone below would glance up in his direction, aware that they were being watched. They did not find offence in his all-seeing gaze, knowing with a sense of comfort that they were being not so much watched as watched over. The people of Danebury often stood in awe of their Chieftain, but above all they loved him for they knew he was a good man. His intentions were always honourable, he cared deeply for his village and its people, took care of them and had also led them in battle to great honour, securing many trophies of war for his brave warriors. Their victories gave the men great standing in their own communities and also among the other peoples of the south lands.

But there was even more than this to their Chieftain, they

knew. He was a strange man, different to all other men who stood upon Dannu's land. It was a great tale to tell around the campfire, of the tall one who had simply walked out of the land one day, bringing the hot summer sun with him and changing forever the lives of those at Dane-bre. Unable even to speak their language or even catch his own food at first, he had filled the people with distrust and fear. He did not look like any other man or act like any other man. Even the clothing he wore and the equipment he carried was like nothing ever seen before.

All the 'normal' men of the times were between five and five foot four in height and generally of a stocky build. The women were even shorter. Parrish in stark contrast stood over six feet in his Army issue combat boots, towering above all others. The people of Danebury had witnessed strange feats and odd actions that they could not explain and the holy one of the village had thus come to the undeniable conclusion that Parrish was very special. Sent from out of the land with all his strange ways and powers to guide the people of Danebury through their lives on the land of his mistress, Dannu the Earth Goddess. This reasoning had been borne out by the tall man's closeness with Dannu, witnessed several times by many people of the village who then saw the truth of the holy man's words. When he was safely out of earshot the people often referred to Parrish, Chieftain of Dane-bre, as Dannu's man.

Parrish knew nothing of his people's close association of him with their Goddess. It *was* true however that he was very aware of their deep religious convictions and had even witnessed first-hand the power of the Earth Goddess on several occasions. But those things were beyond both his control and often comprehension, and so he concentrated his efforts on the preservation and advancement of his village. It was sometimes a heavy burden to carry but one that he had accepted gladly when the people had asked him to be their leader. He did not know they saw him as Dannu's man but knew they trusted his dedication to and love for their village. It was a well-founded trust and they were happy give him ultimate power over them, for a Chieftains word was final.

Parrish was also aware that in some aspects of running a village he was woefully inadequate, not having been born and raised in the times in which he now lived. But to guide him whenever he faltered or was undecided he had friends to turn to. Good friends. And also his wife.

He could not directly ask his diminutive wife Juli for advice of course. Women here were grossly subservient to the warriors in Neolithic times, being the workhorses of the village. It was not done for a warrior, let alone a Chieftain, to ask or even consider a mere female opinion. But he still valued her opinion when spoken in the privacy of their own home. His main collaborator, in times of indecision and matters of village protocol, was his very good friend, right hand man and brave battle warrior Klud.

The two men had once fought against each other but even though Klud had been thoroughly defeated, he bore no malice towards the greater man and in subsequent adventures together their friendship had grown into a tight bond no other man could break. Each could, and had before, trust the other with his very life.

Parrish counted himself a very lucky man and felt satisfied with his life among the people of the Earth Goddess. Only occasionally did he feel the pang of regret at never being able to return to the time of his birth in the late twentieth century. He knew he did not miss the excesses of that time with its pollution, fast vehicles, fast food and decadent, directionless and lazy lifestyle. But he did sometimes miss terribly the friends he had left behind, and would have dearly liked to see his parents just one more time. But that was not possible for all those things were yet to be, some 5,500 years ahead in the distant future. And so Parrish brought his attention sharply back to the time at hand.

Things had not gone too badly.

The winter had certainly been cold enough but there had not been much snow. Two of his villagers had unfortunately died from the cold and related illness. He felt sorry for the families who had followed the holy man up to the little knoll in the east where the bodies of the dead were offered up to the sky spirits. Those black birds who it was believed would carry off their souls to the great shrine house of the Earth Goddess to await rebirth. But the others of Danebury just counted their loss as acceptable, believing without question that the deaths were the wishes of Dannu, and simply carried on with their own lives with scant regard for the private grief of those close to the deceased.

The Chieftain of Danebury stood at his threshold for a few

moments more before turning and going into his house. Even though the day had been fine, with the land beginning to warm now the early spring days grew longer, his keen eye had been acutely aware of the darkening sky away on the far horizon.

There was a storm coming and judging by the already dark colour of the ugly smudge of cloud low in the distance, it was going to be a bad one.

Passing through the storage-cum-fuel store that made up the first third of his oblong shaped cabin, he swept aside the inner door blanket that momentarily barred his way into the square living quarters. The solid, sturdy building had been built by his own hands, although helped in no small part by others of Danebury who were more than willing to show their gratitude and pay in kind for the help he had given in earlier times. Built entirely from interlocking logs as opposed to the more usual wattle and daub construction of Neolithic huts, it bore little resemblance to any other building in Danebury apart from the thatch on its roof. Inside, the bulbous, wide mouthed fireplace, bed platform raised up off the floor and table with four stools, all the like of which had never been seen before by the people of the village, filled Parrish with pride and gave him a feeling of warmth. But all this came a distant second to the glow he felt at the sight that met his eyes and filled his heart as he entered his home.

Juli sat upon the edge of the bed platform, naked from the waist up. With her swollen breasts she was an even more magnificent picture of womanhood than usual but even this did not thrill him as much as the sight of the small baby she suckled at one breast.

His son.

The tiny boy meant everything not just to Parrish and his wife, but also to all of his people. Even almost a year on, everyone could still vividly remember the tragedy, agony and deadly fury that befell their tall leader after the terrible loss of Juli's first baby, miscarried in the field. There had been tears shed, blood spilled and a lot of suffering endured before the Chieftain could come to terms with the grim event and his own mistakes. Thus the birth of an heir to the tall man was a cause great celebration.

Parrish was almost beside himself with joy as he witnessed the birth, something the attendant women of Danebury felt was an extraordinary thing. Warriors never paid attention to such things. But then they in particular knew Parrish was not like any warrior who had ever been before:

Juli was so happy to have finally given the man who was her husband a son, and the village itself was jubilant that not only had Dannu given their Chieftain a baby to honour her, continuing both his line and the presence of people upon her land, but that it was a boy baby and possibly heir to his strange powers. The holy one had happily blessed the newborn one, taking him still bloody from his mother’s womb and going out into the world and raising him aloft. He showed the child to Dannu, to her wondrous world in all its beauty, and also to the waiting people of Dane-bre who were gathered outside. At his presentation a great cheer erupted from the crowd, made all the louder because it was a boy as well as the son of a Chieftain. Inside, Parrish and Juli heard the cheer and held each other tightly, still grinning like idiots when their son was returned, so full were they with pride.

Parrish approached the two people dearest to him in the whole world, gently cupped the babes head in one hand and smiled down at his wife, who smiled adoringly back. He recalled her concern when the holy one had asked for a name for the boy. Parrish had said he wished him called after an old and valued friend he had once known but would never see again. No one else knew of his former life, save one who was not of Danebury, and Juli was suddenly worried that, if like the other words her husband spoke when he was in deep thought, words no one else understood and Parrish had once told her was in a language called 'English', then the baby would have an unpronounceable, meaningless name. Her concern was soon quelled on hearing his reason for the baby’s name. If this unknown person had been a good friend of her husbands, then he must have been a great warrior too, she reasoned. To everyone's satisfaction the boy was given a good, simple, short and what the holy one decreed was an honest sounding name.

“How is Chris?" The proud father asked.

“Chris is hungry, as always." his wife replied. The name would take a while to become familiar but she liked the sound of it anyway. Her Gaelic/Celtic pronunciation gave it more of a guttural 'K' as in Klud, but the meaning of the name was still not lost on Parrish. To hear the word was to remind him of his soldier partner and co-member of B squad in their platoon when they were both proud, well trained fighting men of the 2nd Battalion the Light Infantry.

Chris Dunn, 'Clive' to his muckers, had been with Parrish throughout most of his eight years in Her Majesties Forces and they had become great friends.

His friendly banter, good hearted mickey taking and solid friendship was a cheery and reassuring anchor in the sometimes turbulent, hard and aggressive world of the front line British soldier. The military way was still with Parrish along with all its associated training and skills. Skills that were ingrained into him through years of rigorous training and often came to the surface, especially in times of stress or battle.

The couple stared at each other for a moment, the love light burning brightly in their eyes.

“I thought you ought to know." Parrish spoke quietly. "There is a storm coming from the east. Make any preparations you might need for it."

“When I have finished feeding the baby?" She put it as a question, still finding some difficulty in coming to terms with the relaxed attitude the tall man had with the women of the time. Any other man would have meant the sentence as an instruction that was to be followed immediately, for women did the bidding of their men, their masters, without question or pause. To do otherwise would invoke swift punishment for such unpardonable insubordination.

“Of course." was Parrish’s simple reply. "I will go and make sure the rest of the village also knows the storm is on its way."

He kissed the baby’s head, then kissed Juli on the mouth before leaving the cabin to hurry off down towards the village proper.

Juli simply shook her head in wonderment. She knew he was on his way to keep the people informed because he cared for them, but did he not understand that they were sure to be aware of the approaching weather long before he could tell them? There were still many things he did not know about those he ruled over but they in turn did not mind his ignorance of what to them were simple facts of life. It was part of what made him the man he was and the simple acts he did were proof, if proof were needed, that his was a genuine concern for all their welfare, and it endeared him to them all the more.

2

The whole event was quite nasty for a spring storm. It lasted a lot longer than expected too.

Rain lashed down in an almost constant torrent for a whole day and night while strong, gusty winds rushed across the land and cut through the hillfort.

Few people ventured out and the village was quickly reduced to a mud swamped ghost town.

The sheep huddled as best they could out of the worst of the conditions by tucking themselves under the cover of the edge of the forest canopy, what there was of it this early in the year, or else trying to hide behind some of the outbuildings near the still barren crop fields.

Parrish stood beneath the shelter of the entrance porch of the Chieftains hut, his official residence in the village proper, along with the holy man and they both watched the hard rain slanting down to drive with firm splashes into the puddled, muddied earth.

“A bad storm, my Chieftain." said the smaller man simply. An innocent enough remark unless you knew the little shaman well. He could be a man of few words but all of them direct in instruction or enigmatic in religion. Parrish knew that when the man commented on the storm being bad, he more exactly meant that it was unusual.

"It is a bit severe, I'll agree." he replied. "But surely it is just the last of the big winter blows?"

“Winter storms have all blown their last long before the time to seed the earth is at hand. And that time is now upon us, Parrish. I tell you now that if it does not stop soon, I will begin to wonder what we have all done to incur the wrath of Dannu.”

The last statement was a bit of a shock to the tall man. Although he had really only glimpsed the real power of the Earth Goddess he knew, and more importantly felt, that she was wise and good and fair. She could not, would not punish the people upon her land without good reason and he knew the people of Danebury were honest, good and true to her. They did not deserve and had certainly not earned themselves any extra hardship. Life here in the land before time could be hard enough. His people needed that wheat crop in the late summer to help sustain them through the next winter. He looked down at the religious shaman and rested a hand lightly on his shoulder.

"I am sure she has no cause for anger. The storm will pass." He hoped he sounded confident.

The holy man nodded. Words spoken from Dannu's man were as good as words from Dannu herself. He spoke without looking up at the great man.

“When it is clear again the fields must be allowed a few good days to dry out because then they must be seeded, for it is time. The people must be told and I have many preparations to make.” Then he looked up into the strong face and Parrish smiled before nodding his dismissal. The shaman nodded back in respect, the only man who did not have to properly bow to the Chieftain, then turned and dashed out into the rain, heading off towards the largest building in the village, the central shrine hut.

Parrish stared after him through the grim weather. He had a bad feeling in the pit of his stomach. The holy man had almost as good as said that something was not right. Not right with Dannu and that meant not right with the world. His people and all the other people on the planet were at the mercy of the natural elements. Elements which were held in balance by the Earth Goddess. If that balance was lost all control was gone. A sudden fear gripped him as he realized that if things continued to go badly on the weather front, there was precious little he or anyone else could do about it. He knew too that two or three bad seasons on the trot would just about do for the people of Danebury.

And most probably all the other villages that were dotted throughout the southlands, he concluded. They all lived a subsistence existence, taking each season as it came and rolling on from one year to the next. If a very bad season meant a poor crop, bad grazing and therefore a detrimental effect on all their food supplies, he could see his village rapidly approaching the brink of the slippery slope to starvation, deprivation, disintegration and death. Suddenly he had never felt so helpless. An involuntary shudder ran down his spine and it wasn't because of the chill wind. His eyes went up towards where his cabin sat atop the knoll. It was actually invisible through the grey curtain of rain but he still pictured his wife and young son, snug inside. They too were at risk if Mother Nature did not for some reason run her natural course.

He felt and urgent need to go to them and steeled himself momentarily before, just as the holy man had, he dashed out into the downpour and sloshed rapidly through the clinging mud on the way up towards his home.

The rains finally relented and the villagers held their breath for the next few days while the weather stabilized, allowing the soil to dry enough to be seeded. In fact the ground dried out rather nicely because for the following days the sun burned brightly. Some might even say it seemed rather too warm for the time of year.

Early on the fourth day the people of Danebury were gathered at the edge of the prepared plots. The holy man sang his songs to Dannu then danced energetically around the bare oblongs of tilled earth, lavishing an equal amount of attention and prayer on each and every one in the wish for the ground to give its best and grow forth the biggest and finest crop it could manage. The priceless seed that had been stored in the specially made earthen pots, hermetically sealed and kept in safety behind the great statue of the Earth Goddess, was solemnly handed out and the collective peoples of the village carefully and thoroughly seeded the soil they had hand tilled. The warm weather made them sweat but even so it was joyous work. Seed in the ground would eventually become bread in their mouths. All were eternally grateful for this blessing from

Dannu and so paid the utmost attention to how much, how far apart and how deep the precious seeds were sown.

When the task was completed to everyone's satisfaction, including the shaman and the Chieftain who had watched over the whole proceedings with eagle eyes, everyone retired to the great shrine hut where more prayers were sung before a low key celebration sealed the day, this annual event somehow setting the seal on the full arrival of spring in the minds of the people. They finally drifted off to their beds, tired but happy.

This joy did not last. Two days later the unpredictable weather changed again. For the worse. There wasn't another storm, but it clouded over and once more began to rain. And just kept on raining.

After a full day of constant rain, the faces of the people of the village showed their worry. The dark sky bore no sign of even a slackening of the deluge, let alone a break in the weather. It continued raining through the night.

The next morning Parrish walked through the wetness down to the nearest plot and studied the sodden ground for several drenched minutes, deep in thought. Those few who had by necessity found themselves out in the rain too watched their Chieftain with undisguised curiosity. After a few moments more he knelt in the mud and plunged his hand into the mire digging deep with his fingers he pulled out of the wet ground a fistful of the rich soil and probed it with his index finger. From the bottom of the sod he plucked free one of the freshly sewn seed. It was still firm but it didn't take much wisdom to see that not too much more rain would begin to rot the grains before they had a chance to germinate.

Throwing the earth down at his feet he spun on his heel and strode purposefully back into the hillfort, watched now by even more of his people. Quickly calling his warriors, who gathered around him, he told them what to do. They were confused and unsure at first, until he explained why. The explanation was a gift to the men they knew, for a Chieftain had no need to do this. His word was final and beyond question. To a man they were grateful for Parrish’s gift and the enlightenment and hope it brought.

At the great man's word the warriors dispersed and instructed their womenfolk to bring out of their houses all the woven straw mats they possessed. These mats were the basis of all the floors, work areas and bedding within every single living quarter inside Danebury hillfort. Woven from the dried stems of bygone crops, the mats had a hundred and one different uses from basic floor coverings to temporary wall or roofing repairs.

Why would the Chieftain want all the mats in the village? Did he not know it would make the lives of everyone that much more uncomfortable?

The whole village turned out once again, as Parrish knew it would without him having to order it, to stand in the pouring rain to do their Chieftains bidding. Even the holy man and the Chieftain's own wife were present, clutching their own bundles of straw mats under their arms. Even those who could supply no mats, the older ones and the children, had come to see what on earth Parrish intended to do with them all.

On earth was indeed the correct term.

“My people." Parrish addressed the crowd above the soft sound of the falling rain. It could not dampen the tone of warmth that was in his voice as he looked upon them. "The rain does not show any sign of stopping. I know you do not understand why I have asked you for your floor coverings but I would not do such a thing without good reason."

There were several nods from the crowd.

“If the rain does not stop soon the seeds we planted not long ago will be washed away or rot where they lay." This time the reaction was one of gasps as the enormity of his statement struck home. They all had their suspicions but to hear it directly from the mouth of Dannu's man meant it was undeniably true.

"So, I would ask you now to all give up your matting and help me to cover all the ground that we have seeded." There was no doubt they would do as he asked but Parrish still put it as an offer to satisfy his own set of morals, different in so many ways to all the others around him.

"The matting will help to protect the ground and the seed, keep off some of the rain and hold the soil together and prevent it from washing away."

The sea of faces before him nodded, although he doubted many of them genuinely understood his reasoning. Never-the-less, they were immediately keen on carrying out their

Chieftains wish, which was without doubt offered up to help if at all possible the suddenly very real danger he had just pointed out to them.

The crowd, soaked to the skin already, surged out through the great gate and immediately set to work as instructed. They cover the tilled fields with the mats, using short stakes or split sticks to securely peg down the edges of each one.

Unfortunately, as many as there seemed to be when they were all collected together, the woven matting was not sufficient to cover all the fields although the bulk of them were soon under their protective coverage. Parrish quickly gave orders for a number of the smaller outbuildings, those miniature storage huts that were satellites to the people's main living quarters inside the village, to be taken apart and the thatch from their roofs and wattle from the walls used to cover the rest. The little huts could quickly and easily be rebuilt, and as far as he was concerned the survival of the crops came first.

The old flint knapper was first to offer his storage hut into the hands of the wreckers, more than glad to help, saying with a wry smile that if the hut was gone he would have easier access to some of those good flint nodules that had until now been inaccessible, at the rear of the hut. Parrish clapped him warmly on the back, sharing a smile with him. The Neolithic man epitomized the fighting spirit that all his people possessed in times of trouble.

With the crop ground finally protected from the worst ravages of the weather, the people of Danebury returned to their homes to dry out. Parrish alone stood on in the rain for several long moments, apparently lost in his thoughts. The villagers knew when this happened that he was trying to communicate with his mistress. They all hoped he was asking her what they had done wrong to deserve such hardship and if it were at all possible for them to put right the mysterious wrong.

Parrish himself was simply wondering if his rough and ready idea would work, and how any other villages were coping if they too were suffering, as his own people were?

3

The weather continued to remain unsettled. The next few days still showed no sun and the rain, although now more intermittent, often fell heavily and continued to churn the ground to mud. All the people could do watch in helpless dismay.

Then the rain did stop. But there was to be no respite. The villagers were amazed to see the brooding sky begin to turn even darker than before, bulbous black clouds rolling in from the east. Next the wind died away and the land then seemed to be holding its breath, still and hushed, and everyone became aware of the tingling of the skin and that feeling of a heaviness in the air that unmistakably signaled an impending electrical storm.

Parrish fully understood such atmospheric effects, his twentieth century knowledge able to explain away the great crashes of rolling thunder, the blinding illuminations of the sky from sheet lightning and the occasionally seen zig-zags of light that were thunderbolts stabbing down into the earth and searching out the best conductors to unload their power through. Tall trees, buildings, metallic objects, although there were of course none upon the land now, or even simply the high ground. Whatever afforded the easiest routes for the bolts to deliver their charge to the ground.

But Parrish could not explain these things to his village. Like all simple folk, they cowered in fear at the unknown and in any case, to attempt to reason the storm away with logic would be to deny the people their religion. As far as they were concerned the soon to be released elemental forces were sent directly from Dannu. She controlled the living earth, the sky and everything between the two. How furious she must be to send such an angry sky! Yet no one could understand why. What had they all done to warrant such punishment? The holy one received many searching glances. No direct questions would be asked of him out of respect, but a lot could be said with just a look. The little man felt the pressure and he also dreaded the coming storm.

It was in the afternoon, although no one could be exactly sure because there was no visible sun to tell by its position if it had yet passed its zenith that the storm arrived. It rolled unstoppably across the shadowed land, rumbling thunder announcing its approach.

Parrish had hoped it might pass over the village before fully breaking but it was not to be. Just a few kilometers short of Danebury and plainly going to cross directly overhead, the black clouds began to deliver their dramatic goods. The thunder crashed with enough percussion to make buildings tremble.

Some families cowered inside their huts but many people, and not just the warriors, seemed to gather around their Chieftains hut where Parrish stood beneath its thatched awning, watching. He wasn't sure whether it was a conscious thing on their part but it was as if they drew close to him for protection. From the storm or Dannu, he wondered?

Sheet lightening lit up the edges of the thunder clouds from within, their momentary flashes throwing the dulled and darkened countryside into stark relief. There was real fear beginning to show on the faces of those around their Chieftain now and he attempted to quell them with a smile, gathering as many of the women and children as he could into the shelter beneath his porchway.

Those in the crowd who had fine hair found it beginning to float out from their scalps to stand eerily on end. If there was enough ionization in the air to produce that effect Parrish knew what was to come.

“There will be thunderbolts.” he said simply.

As if his words were the cue, the first bolt flashed white in the sky, stabbing jaggedly down into the forest only a short distance way, no doubt wreaking havoc on some tall tree within its depths. Scant moments later the village was rocked by a tremendous clap of thunder that made even Parrish flinch. Another bolt lanced down away at the far edge of the storm. This was followed by more rolling thunder and a number of sheet lightning flashes. The air hung close and heavy and Parrish actually found himself wishing it would rain once more and relieve the weight of the oppressive air.

Then the storm was overhead.

The black, angry sky seemed almost low enough to be touched.

Expected, and yet without warning, a bolt flashed down near the village, to the horror of the people striking into the burial knoll off to the east of the village. It was no doubt attracted to the raised trestles on that little peak of high ground. It was only then that Parrish really feared for his village. Being a hillfort, it was quite naturally sited atop a hill, making them a prime target, with his own cabin at the highest point being the most obvious point of strike. He felt no dismay at the prospect of his house being destroyed. Juli and Chris were with him now and he would gladly sacrifice his cabin if the rest of his people could be spared.

Lightning flashed, thunder roared and the simple villagers cowered. Those inside their huts tried to close their ears to the assault while those gathered at their Chieftains side marveled at the way he refused to cower before Dannu, standing defiant and tall in the face of her anger. The sky raged above like never seen before, yet he remained calm and steady below.

That was until the very next lightning strike.

Everyone instinctively ducked as, with a simultaneous clap of thunder that stunned the senses; a jagged line of dazzling, pure white electrical power stabbed from the churning sky and struck a family hut not fifty meters from where they were all standing.

Parrish had seen the destructive effects of explosions many times during his tours of Northern Ireland while serving with the Light Infantry. Like everyone around him he watched in both silent horror and morbid fascination at the spectacle before them. There was no sound of detonation but the resulting effect was the same. As the lightening released its tremendous power in a single moment into the roof of the hut, the dwelling just seemed to fly apart as if blasted from the inside. The roof thatching was flung far and wide, the wattle and daub walls disintegrated and the supporting spars of the roof and the main structuring timbers collapsed in on themselves.

“My house!" was all Narn could gasp from beside Parrish as he stared in dismay at how what only seconds before had been the building housing his family, was in an instant reduced to nothing more than match wood, a great scattering of straw and a jumbled mass of broken and charred spars.

Littered among the rubble were visible some of the effects of those who had occupied it.

Still occupied it!

Amazingly, from among the wreckage stumbled a totally dazed woman clutching her baby tight in her arms. Both were miraculously unharmed but neither could make a single sound, so shocked and wide eyed with terror were they.

"Shit!" shouted Parrish in English and dashed from under the porch, across the soggy ground and through the scattered wreckage to help the poor unfortunates.

The others followed him at the run, as much to stay within Dannu's man’s protection as to help anyone else who might be trapped in the rubble.

Parrish met the woman and child, steered them towards a cluster of women behind the warriors at his back, then leapt into the wreckage in search of more survivors. The anger of the storm was forgotten to him now. It rolled on, moving now beyond the hillfort as if satisfied that it had caused sufficient damage, destruction and dismay, yet still thrusting occasional fingers of angry light and power into the defenseless earth.

The Chieftain, watched with curiosity by the women who stood off to one side, started urgently turning over or throwing aside pieces of timber, sections of walling or loose and flapping bedding skins in search of survivors. The other warriors caught his drift and began searching also, even though they didn't quite understand why. To their way of thinking the damage and any accompanying deaths had already been done.

A second child, weeping quietly, was quickly found and pulled out from beneath a low section of wall that had somehow survived the impact. The child was handed into the grateful arms of the woman who had managed to stagger free moments earlier but the babies actual mother, who had protected her offspring from the bulk of the fallen wall with her own body, had not been so lucky. Parrish looked sadly down at the crushed, still form that had given its life in protection of the babe, and shook his head. He was about to go to Narn, who was busy searching the tangled mass that used to be the other side of the hut, with the bad news of one of his wives death, when the warrior in question let out a cry and unceremoniously pulled free from the debris the limp body of a young man. It was laid gently down on a patch of open ground among the wreckage and everyone began to gather around.

Parrish quickly joined the crowd, was allowed free passage through to the front and then knelt beside the prostrate adolescent.

"He is dead, my Chieftain." said Nam quietly. "My son." The warrior was determined not to show weakness in front of the others of Dane-bre but the last words caught in his throat and he stared hard down at his boy on the ground, unwilling to allow the tears in his eyes to be seen.

The boy, perhaps thirteen of fourteen summers old, seemed to be totally unmarked in death. Parrish rested a hand gently on the still chest. He was about to offer his condolences to Narn when he thought he detected one brief beat beneath his palm. Putting his ear to the chest he waved the crowd to silence and listened. There appeared to be no further sign but he was sure he'd felt something. Could the boy have just been stunned into arrest by the harsh jolt of electricity?

Parrish wasted no time. He started CPR.

All the rest of the villagers stared in silent amazement as their Chieftain pushed violently onto the boy's chest then tilted the head back and began to blow his own breath into the still body.

Fifteen chest compressions between each pair of breaths. Parrish remembered the sequence from his first aid training. It was compulsory for every soldier to know the basic ABC resuscitation techniques.

He had been working furiously on the unresponsive youngster for almost half a minute before the crowd began to recover their composure on witnessing his strange antics.

“But ... he is dead, Parrish." It was Klud, the only man with nerve enough to correct the Chieftain in front of his people, and then only because he was his close personal friend. He alone spoke but voiced the one thought in all their heads. Surely it was not right to assault a body so after it was dead? Plus, he was one of Dane-bre's own and so clearly did not deserve such bad treatment.

Parrish could not spare the time to reply and so ignored the almost apologetically spoken words, continuing his heart massage for a few moments more before stopping to feel the side of the boy’s neck. The Carotid artery pulsed. Yes, a heartbeat!

Tilting the young head back once more he resumed his rhythmic blowing into the mouth, watching the chest deflate naturally as it exhaled after each breath. Parrish himself was now quite breathless from his exertions but continued, the recommended rate being twelve to sixteen a minute, as he had been taught by the Royal Army Medical Corps instructors. The tall man got no further than the sixth breath.

Like the bump starting of an unreliable engine, the boy suddenly caught, jerked spasmodically then convulsed into a tremendous coughing fit. He gulped in great draughts of air and was racked once more with coughs before opening his eyes, surprised to find himself clutched in the arms of his Chieftain. One last hack and he sat slowly up, eyes wide in his head as the Chieftain sat back on his haunches with a satisfied grin on his face, while everyone else gathered around him just stared, agog.

“What ... what has happened?" he ventured in a whisper.

Parrish helped the boy to his feet. He swayed unsteadily and the tall man supported him by the shoulders.

“Steady now, you took a bit of a shock from the lightning strike but you are OK now." he said then beckoned Narn forward. "Your son." he added with a smile.

Narn, along with Klud, Juli and all the others of Danebury, were still frozen in amazement. Was his son really alive? All eyes were now on the tall man. The strange man. Dannu's man.

The boy had been dead. They were sure, had all seen his closed eyes, the still chest. Yet Parrish had then breathed his own breath into the boy's mouth and somehow brought him back to life. It was not possible and yet they had all just seen it done! Did the Chieftain have the power of life within him, as well as the power of death which everyone had more than once seen dispensed with ruthless efficiency?

Nam slowly held out his arms.

“Son?"

The boy moved to his father and they embraced quickly before recovering their composure and stepping stiffly apart, a more fitting stance in public for a warrior and his eldest son although a caring hand was permitted to steady the miraculously recovered youngster. Neither could suppress their grins though.

"Do not worry about your house." Parrish told them both as if nothing untoward had just happened. "When the storms are past we will join together in the re-building of it. You can have the shelter of my round hut until the work is done."

Nam nodded gratefully and everyone else nodded too in appreciation and acknowledgment. Parrish grinned.

“And now would be a good time to go to your homes. Quickly," He glanced up at the heavens. “I think the clouds are about to break once more. It is going to rain."

The people did as ordered and began to disperse. Nam and his boy were led away to the body of his wife, where they somberly set about taking care of her, helped, as was right and proper, by the holy man.

Juli waited patiently behind her husband and watched with intense curiosity as Klud stepped up close to his tall friend. The Neolithic man waited till all the others had gone before he spoke and Juli, as discretely as she could, leant her full attention to the warrior's words.

“That was truly the most wondrous thing I have ever seen." he said, his features gravely serious. "You are indeed a great man, my Chieftain."

Parrish clapped Klud reassuringly on the arm.

"I tell you now my friend, doing 'the kiss of life', for that is what it is called, is not always successful. The boy was fortunate he had not actually been struck by the lightening or any falling timbers and that he was found so quickly. One day, if you like, I could teach you how to do the kiss of life."

Klud shook his head.

“I do not think so. That magic must remain yours and yours alone." Parrish laughed out loud at the idea of CPR as magic.

“As you wish, my friend." He clapped the man warmly on the shoulder. "Go to your family now and we will speak no more of it."

Klud bowed deeply to his Chieftain and moved away, knowing that despite his words people would be speaking about the latest supernatural feat of Dannu's man for a long time to come.

Parrish watched his friend go and found himself alone with his wife and young son among the wreckage of the destroyed hut. She came to his side and hugged him, her free hand snaking around his waist while the other hugged her baby close. Little Chris had remained silent throughout the whole event. He smiled down at them both and she returned the warm gesture. Her husband never ceased to amaze and impress and she sometimes felt that he was truly capable of anything.

“That was a great thing, my husband, to bring someone back from the dead.” she paused for a moment, choosing her words carefully before continuing. Not only was she about to ask him a question, but she also intended to question his actions, something she'd never done before. After all, he was the Chieftain and his word was final. How would he respond to direct scrutiny?

"Do you ... do you think that Dannu would approve? I mean, taking back from her a soul she had prepared for offering up to the sky spirits?"

Parrish, unaware that the thinly disguised direct query to his actions could be construed as offensive to him, shook his head.

“No. She would not have allowed me to revive the boy if it had truly been his time to go to her.” He put an arm lovingly around her shoulders. "But let us speak no more of it now. Here is not the place. Come, back to the cabin, I am sure it is about to rain."

As the words left his lips the first spots of moisture hit the ground with heavy wet slaps. Thunder rolled one more time away in the middle distance and as the family moved hastily up the slope towards the only square structure in the village, the rain started once more in earnest. Grey sheets of it came sweeping in across the forest to engulf the hillfort, pattering down on the thatching and splashing angrily against the surfaces of the woven mats that dared to deny the bright drops their attacks on the seeded fields.

Parrish was asked the very same question again the next morning by the holy man, and again gave the same answer. The shaman too seemed satisfied with the reply and then broached the subject that he had originally come to the Chieftain to discuss.

"The woman killed in the lightning strike ..."

“One of Narn's wives.” interrupted Parrish, trying to put a more human element into the subject. He felt guilty that even now he did not know the poor woman's name. “... needs to be offered up to the sky spirits." The smaller man continued, ignoring the trivial interruption. "But the burial mound was also struck yesterday. With your permission I would like to take some men to help me with the rebuilding of any trestles that might be either damaged or destroyed."

“Let us both go and see what damage there is.” offered Parrish, unwilling to take men from the building of Narn's house unless necessary. He wanted the hut rebuilt quickly and to take people away would look as if he was reneging on his promise of swift reconstruction, made only one day before.

The holy man nodded his satisfaction at the suggestion and together they strolled out of the hillfort and made their way up towards that little knoll in the east, glad of the un-muddied grass that made the going underfoot somewhat easier.

The sight that greeted them there only dismayed the Chieftain but it deeply shocked the shaman and he stood back, not wanting to go any nearer than necessary.

Most of the trestles had suffered at least some damage from the blast, several being completely destroyed, but what really rattled the little Neolithic man were the bodies littering the ground. Not the charred and scattered remains of the single human cadaver that had occupied a trestle, but the half dozen or so dead birds that had obviously taken shelter from the storm among the timber struts and had all been killed by the strike.

Parrish himself really couldn't care less about the death of a few carrion crows but he knew their significance to everyone else in this land. They were the much revered sky spirits, creatures sent by Dannu to strip the carcasses of their flesh and in the process carry away their souls on their jet black wings. Carry them away back to the Earth Goddess who held them in safety until the time was right for rebirth.

The holy man was for several long moments at a loss for words and Parrish took charge.

“Do not tell anyone of this." He said quietly. “I will clear away the bodies of the spirits and repair all the trestles myself so no one else need come here until it is as before."

“But ... but I do not understand, Parrish. What is happening?" A look of total bewilderment filled the little shaman's face. "The storms, the rains, Narn's house, his wife and now this. I *know* the Earth Goddess would not strike down her people without good reason. We have done nothing to deserve such punishment and as for her treatment of the spirits. Well,” he paused before actually criticizing his god. "I know that this is not right.”

It was unprecedented for a holy one to say such a thing and all the tall man could do was shake his head. He could offer no explanation.

“It is beyond me also. But like you my friend, I would dearly like to know what in Dannu's name is going on.”

“I might be able to help you with that.” came a dry, rusty voice from behind them. "And in time you might be able to help us.” it added when, as one the pair spun in amazement to seek out the source of that unmistakable sound.

Trailing away from them down the slope towards the flatter ground below was a long entourage of perhaps twenty or thirty holy men, all who had approached without warning. At the head of this human snake, assisted by a man on either side, was an old, wizened and grey haired yet eagle eyed man.

Both the Danebury men knew who he was. In fact, *everybody* knew who he was but only a few had ever seen him in the flesh. Yet here he now stood, the oldest of the wise ones and head of the holy village behind the great stone temple of Dannu. He had travelled across the southlands, the infirmity of his great age making it a difficult journey of at least four days, to the village of Dane- bre.

Before them stood the great, high priest of the religion of the Earth Goddess.

4

After the initial shock of the arrival of the holiest of the holy ones had washed over and staggered the people of Dane-bre, they were then almost falling over themselves to do whatever they possibly could for their revered religious leader. He who they believed without doubt was in contact with Dannu at all times. To please him was to please her.

Parrish let his people carry on, fetching, carrying and generally assisting their honoured guests however they saw fit. It *was* a great honour for them he realized, but privately wondered how long the visitors intended to stay. If his village spent too much time tending to the needs of the holy ones, it would disrupt the longer term lives of the villagers.

The wisest of the wise ones was offered accommodation in the Chieftains stall inside the great shrine hut, which he accepted graciously enough, and the others of his entourage automatically took residence in all the other stalls.

The Chieftain gave them most of the rest of the day to get settled, fed and rested, while he occupied his time with repairing the trestles on the knoll, with limited help from a few of his warriors. He would not let them visit the site itself but was glad of their help in felling the young trees for the free standing constructions. He noted with a wry smile that the villages own holy man, who would normally be directly involved with such religious work, was glaringly absent, but that too was understandable. He also needed to attend his visiting peers, betters and of course their leader, all who were now guests in his own holy house.

Naturally, whenever something strange happened, as it now seemed to be doing with unnerving regularity around the tall man, tongues wagged. And not just among the women.

“It is a great honour to have the holy ones visit us.” said Tomps as the small band of warriors busied themselves felling straight trunks for the legs of the new trestles.

“That is true enough.” agreed Klud, his large, flint headed felling axe biting deep into the column of a knotty pine. "I have never heard of such a visit happening before."

“That is what I thought.” said Parrish without the enthusiasm so evident in all the others. “They are clearly here for a reason and it is probably an important one. It cannot have been an easy journey through the bad weather. And the great wise one is a very old man. Something extra special has caused him to come all the way out here."

The other warriors stopped working and listened to their Chieftains words in silence. The tall man was right of course, but what reasoning! Proof again, if proof were needed, that Parrish was truly a clever man. A man who could see far.

“I think that it will have something to do with you, my friend." Even Klud's more limited intelligence could work that one out.

"Yes." said Parrish bluntly, heaving a pine spar onto his shoulder with a grunt. "And no doubt they'll get around to telling me what it is in their own good time." he grumbled under his breath as he set off back towards the hillfort.

The sky remained grey and miserable but had managed not to disgorge any more rain so far.

It was late in the afternoon when a young runner was dispatched to the Chieftains hut. Parrish was there, talking with Klud about the slow but steadily progressing work on Narn's house. The temporarily homeless warrior and his family were now settled in their new, greatly honoured residence and so the two men were standing politely outside, although still under the porchway, as was normal protocol when in close proximity to a warrior’s house.

The boy, who was very proud to carry a message from the holy ones, stepped hesitantly up before those he considered the two greatest men in the village, bowed very deeply then said loudly.

“The wise one asks that you go to him. He says he has things to speak with you about.”

“Tell him we are on our way." Parrish replied and waved the lad away, surprised at the sudden annoyance he felt that the holy ones could just stroll up and, simply with their presence, immediately rob him of his position of power as head of his own village. He dismissed the thought, making a mental note to keep a tighter rein on his ego. A self-mocking grin crossed his face. If he wasn't careful, he'd start believing his own press.

“Come on Klud, it looks like we are about to find out just what all this is about."

The two friends entered the shrine hut and strode purposefully around the hearth of the central fire to where the grey haired old man waited patiently for them in front of the Chieftains stall. Parrish walked boldly because he considered Danebury his turf and for once knew it was the holy one who was on unfamiliar ground. Klud's firm strides were, in contrast, a bold front to mask his understandable nervousness at coming under the close scrutiny of so many great and revered holy men. They stopped before the old man and the attendants that always seemed to flank him. He welcomed the two friends with a warm smile and a nod. Parrish returned the smile and bowed respectfully, as was expected even of a Chieftain. Klud's lips twitched as he tried to do the same but his nerves betrayed him and the intended smile would not come. He bowed very deeply to the wisest of the wise ones. To his surprise the great man chose to ignore Parrish and turned his full attention on the Neolithic man.

“Stand tall my brave warrior." The dry voice was unmistakable and the quiet power of it pulled him upright. “We here are honoured by yourpresence.”

All the other holy men, watching in silence, nodded agreement and bowed lightly from the waist. This wide gesture of respect threw Klud completely and he stammered a confused reply.

“But ... but, I ... I am just a humble warrior, doing my best to serve my Chieftain, my village and Dannu." blurted out the man, now clearly uncomfortable at being the center of everyone's attention.

“Do not be so modest, my friend." The old man stepped forward and laid one gnarled hand gently on a muscular shoulder. “You are well known to us, Klud of Dane-bre. We have watched you and are proud of your good deeds."

“My ... my deeds?!" Klud was puzzled, and also shocked that the holy men of Dannu had even bothered to take the time to 'watch' him. He didn't understand why. "But my deeds are nothing compared to Parr .. my Chieftain's." He looked desperately to his tall friend for support and somehow found it in his companion's sudden smile of appreciation.

"Your deeds are as good and important as your Chieftains." corrected the wise one gently. "For you are his right hand. You guide him when he needs it. You help him, fight alongside him and, if need be, you would die with him or for him. No man could ask more of his friend and so Parrish has what few men will ever get." He paused, to allow the importance of the last sentence to sink in.

"Know now Klud, that you increase his strength and are part of what makes him whole. Without you your Chieftain would be less than he now is."

Klud listened to the words in silence, mouth agape, and then turned again to his tall friend who he saw nodding emphatically in agreement.

Parrish too had not realized it fully before but now it had been explained by the holy man he could see it was the truth.

He had always understood, his army training making it clear, that most men were content to be sheep. But there would always be a small number of others who rose above the crowd. They were the ones who really shone. And of these few, some were lights while others were lenses.

Those who fell into the lenses category were not great in themselves but magnified and focused the greatness of the others for the benefit of both, and ultimately for the benefit of all. Clearly Klud was the lens to Parrish's light.

He too laid a grateful arm on the smaller man's shoulder, looked deep into the hawk like eyes beneath the great slash of eyebrows, and grinned widely.

Klud grinned too then and they were for that brief moment locked together once again in their deep and binding friendship. It was a rare moment that all the watching holy men silently appreciated being permitted to see.

“Now you know why they call him the wise one." Parrish said softly and they both laughed, then returned their attention to the subject of the words.

The grey haired man bowed briefly at the compliment then opened his hands apologetically.

“Now I must beg Klud's forgiveness and ask him to leave. What I have to say next is only for the Chieftains ears." He shot Klud a quizzical look.

The Neolithic warrior was not in the least bit offended and bowed deeply to the wise one.

“I understand.” he said, realizing that if just Parrish and the holy men wanted to speak then it obviously involved direct contact with Dannu. This was no place for a mere warrior. He bowed again, this time to both men, then turned and walked boldly away and out of the hut, his chest bursting with pride at the great words and singular attention the wisest of the wise ones had lavished on him.

When the warrior had gone the old man bade Parrish sit and the pair sank to the hard packed earth, one needing some assistance, where they then sat looking at each other for a few long moments.

"It is to do with the weather, is it not?" Parrish ventured eventually.

"In a way, yes."

“Is it bad all over the southlands?"

“Some villages have suffered greatly." The old man nodded sagely. "But the angry skies are worst here. It is to do with you, my tall friend."

“ME?" gasped Parrish in total surprise.

“Yes. The forces in play seem drawn towards you." came the astounding answer. "Because you are from where the forces also come from."

Parrish momentarily gasped, then began to laugh. "You joke with me." he grinned.

"I do not make fun where Dannu is concerned." the old man replied flatly, the expression on his face emphasizing the point.

The smile fell like lead from Parrish’s face. "It is true?" he whispered, incredulously.

A single nod was his answer and the pair fell into a heavy silence. The oldest of the wise ones waited patiently for the question.

“But what am I expected to do?"

“Dannu wants, no needs, your help to find what is causing this badness and make things as they were before."

“Huh?" The Chieftains ignorant sounding grunt was by now well known to mean he did not understand. "And how the blazes am I supposed to do that?"

“Dannu will carry you as near as she can to the place, then you must do whatever you can."

“Oh right." The sarcasm was heavy in Parrish’s voice but somehow he did not dismiss the incredible statement out of hand. The old man seemed very sure of his words and the tall man knew first hand that the Earth Goddess was undeniably powerful and strange things could happen when the holy ones put their minds to it.

Of course! Parrish realized with a jolt. That was it.

“In one of your trances." he said as he understood how he could thus be 'carried' to the trouble. By the strange sort of mesmerism that the holy men could induce with their en-mass chanting and crude light shows. In fact, he had experienced just such a thing once before.

"I understand. And once I have 'seen' this problem of Dannu's, I can tell you how it might be put right.”

“Something like that.” answered the old man in a surprisingly rather non-- committal way. "She will send you and help you when she can. But where you will go her power is weak. You must take care and be prepared."

Parrish nodded and gave a wry smile. To them it were as if he were going on a real journey. No matter. He was quite happy to accommodate the wise one and the odd notions he had. He too then would treat as if it were a real trip, in fact it might be a bit like old times, preparing for an imaginary trek across country. As if readying for an Army exercise, and that was OK because he'd always enjoyed doing that.

“And when does all this 'travelling' take place?"

"This very night, at the high of the moon. Everyone will be ready and you must be too. This shrine hut will be prepared and you must be armed and able to travel fast and light." His tone was deadly serious. " And you of course go with all our best wishes."

Shit, thought Parrish suddenly, he really is taking this thing to heart.

"OK, OK, but I wonder what you seriously expect me to ..."

The sudden sound of Klud, clearing his throat loudly from across the far side of the shrine hut, stopped everything dead. All the holy men, who had been listening intently to the strange, engrossing conversation, had not heard the warrior re-enter and every head turned in his direction.

"You cannot enter here." said one of the men who stood beside the old man. His words were loud and sharp. "This is a meeting of great importance and you have no place ..."

“Quiet!" barked Parrish just as sharply, immediately angry both at seeing his great friend being put down before everyone, and the belittling effect it was having on the usually unflinching warrior. It was as near as he would come to seeing the brave man cower and found the experience deeply upsetting. In stark contrast to Klud's reproachful look, all the holy men now glared openly at the Chieftain of Dane-bre. How dare he? No one treated the servants of Dannu like this.

“What is it Klud?"

“Er ... there is ... there is something you should see·. Outside." As he spoke he once again came under fierce scrutiny and seemed suddenly to find his footwear very interesting rather than look up into the angry faces glowering at him.

“That is hardly something to interrupt the wise one’s words with." It was the same holy man who Parrish had cut short only moments before and this time the Chieftain just ignored him completely.

"Is it very important?" he asked his friend.

“So important that what I have to say must wait?" asked the grey haired old man in a soft yet somehow strong and direct tone.

“I ... I think so." said Klud quietly.

“Then I think so too." said Parrish crisply, cutting short the interrogation. "If my friend and advisor says so, then that is good enough for me. The rest of this talk will have to wait till later."

Without further ado he set off across the hut floor to join the Neolithic warrior. " Lead on." he added as the two met and Klud, seeing his Chieftain daring to rebuke all the holy ones around them to back *him* up, grinned widely at his friend, nodded with gratitude and lead the great man out into the dull and overcast daylight.

All to the slack jawed astonishment of the holy ones.

5

Parrish found all his warriors, armed to a man, standing on the hillfort parapets either side of the main gate. He and Klud climbed up and joined them, gazing out over the defense ditch, the pathway, the animal sheds beyond that and across the open grazing land to the forest beyond.

For there was the focus of everyone's attention.

Along the forests edge, gathering in a dark cluster, were people. Lots of people. Parrish estimated close to hundred and correctly deduced it to be the populous of an entire village.

“They appeared only a short while ago.” Klud informed his Chieftain. “While you were talking inside. What is it they want?" he wondered. "Will they pass on by do you think?"

“That remains to be seen." replied Parrish. “But you were right to call me out. We will watch and wait. I suspect that their leader will at least wish to talk with us."

“Oh.” said Klud quietly. Parrish actually meant that perhaps the strangers would be in need of a few supplies and prepared to barter for them but Klud only remembered the dreadful events that followed the last time his Chieftain had talked with a visiting party of strangers.

The two peoples watched each other intently for a while before a small group detached itself from the crowd among the trees. As they approached slowly across the open ground Parrish counted four men. Three walked in like abreast, one step behind the lead man. A Chieftain and his escort. As they drew nearer it became clear that the only weapons they carried were daggers and clubs or axes, all of which were still tucked into their belts. They approached the hillfort steadily and stopped just out of arrow range, looking expectantly up into the faces along the fort wall.

"Klud, Tomps. With me." was all Parrish said before making his way down towards the main gate. Klud looked at Nam, another warrior who had witnessed the tall one's last parley and what had followed, and they exchanged dubious glances before the two selected warriors followed their Chieftain off the battlements.

At the gate Parrish found all the holy ones gathered there in a tight group behind their leader.

“Is it permitted for one of my people to go with you?" Asked the grey haired old man as the gate was pulled open.

Parrish didn't want to risk the life of one of the keepers of Dannu's temple but understood that the wise one would want to know what was going on.

“I will take Dane-bre's holy man with me, if that is all right with you." he said and received an acknowledging nod and a wry smile. The holy man in question stepped forward. “Keep a few paces back out of the way." was Parrish's immediate advice. “In case of any excitement."

This too received a nod of acknowledgment and the small man fell silently in behind the three warriors and followed their lead as the Chieftain of Danebury lead the way out through the gate to meet with the uninvited strangers.

The group of holy men watched from inside the gate. Danbury's warriors watched from the battlements and the women watched from in front of the Chieftains cabin where they had joined Juli, who watched with trepidation from up on the hillforts high point. The unknown people watched from the forest edge and all seemed to hold their breath as the two small groups at the center of their attention finally came together out on the open ground.

The slate grey sky could contain itself no longer and a fine rain began to fall, slowly wetting the still damp earth and soaking into everyone's clothes. It seemed to lay added hush on to the events happening beneath its sodden clouds.

For long, tense moments the two little warrior bands eyed each other unflinchingly, neither giving an inch in the silent battle of intimidation.

Parrish concentrated on his opposite number, obviously the Chieftain. The man gazing steadily back up at him was of medium Neolithic build, had good, steady features and a firm look. This man was no fool and, unlike the last Chieftain Parrish had encountered, clearly had the best interests of his village uppermost in his mind.

The unknown Chieftain in turn assessed the tall one in the same calculating manner. He took in the almost piercing gaze, the marks on his neck of a *double* Chieftain killer and the towering height. And he knew of the stories. Everyone had heard rumours of the deeds done by the head of Dane-bre. Up to that moment the Chieftain had always dismissed them out of hand as women's talk. Now he was not so sure.

The other warriors from both camps were eyeing each other in more regular terms but in the same aggressive manner. Less evenly matched, being three against two and compounded by the apparently youthfulness of Tomps, the three, although immediately aware of the youngster's tattoos, were also well aware of their numeric superiority and this gave them added confidence.

In a single, masterly stroke Klud quashed the feeling by speaking almost casually across at Tamps.

"You kill yours, I will kill mine. Then I will fight you for the head of the last man."

“Done." said Temps, his tone so deadly serious that the expressions on the faces of the warriors opposite changed immediately from confidence to puzzled uncertainty. The Danebury two just continued to stare on with quietly lethal intent.

Parrish had to suppress a sudden smile of admiration for his friend, and at last addressed the other Chieftain.

“I am Parrish of Dane-be." He felt it unnecessary to say he was Chieftain. "Leave my land and go back to your own village." His voice was level and calm but none the less firm for all that.

The leader of the opposing force was clearly stung at being blatantly told to clear off but protocol demanded a proper reply. The insults and fighting would follow quickly enough.

"I am Shimon, and we have no village."

The answer shocked Parrish and all the rest of his men.

Momentarily forgetting the seriousness of the confrontation he gasped.

“How can that be?"

"A great storm struck us. My village burned to the ground. Some of my people and most of the stock were killed. The crops have been washed away and so I decided to lead my people out."

Shimon found himself explaining his disaster to the tall man without fully realizing why. Perhaps because his opposite number was so imposing a figure, or maybe because he seemed to express a genuine concern. Either way the smaller Chieftain found his grip on the confrontation suddenly slipping and at once attempted to re-assert himself. He got straight to the point.

“We are in search of a new place to live and come in need of many supplies. Give us what we need or we will simply take it."

Everyone stiffened at the outright demand and the blatant threat that underlined it. Parrish understood as well as all the other men around him that there would be killing now. It was the way of these warrior people. Honour and potential loss of face would not allow it any other way. Hands strayed ever nearer to those battle axes and war clubs tucked into belts.

Parrish eyed his opposite for several moments. If his village were attacked many would die. Those people along the tree line must be quite desperate and he knew desperate men fought hard and fought well. The cost to both Shimon's and his own village could very well be high. Too high.

But it didn't have to be so.

“Many would die and there is no need.” he said at last.

A great weight seemed to settle immediately across Klud's shoulders and he eyed his friend as if trying to will him against going down this same road again. He recalled with great sadness the deaths, near disaster and tragedy that had happened the last time his Chieftain spoke this way. Had the great man learned nothing?

Yes, Parrish had indeed learned. He knew there would now have to be death here, but he could still dictate how many. No need this time for a whole village to be wiped out.

“Do not threaten me with your warriors." he continued. "They would all die and without cause. It can be decided another way."

Everyone else was stunned by these surprising words. Confusion reigned on every Neolithic face.

“How?" This time Shimon momentarily forgot the confrontation and asked with genuine curiosity.

"Just me against you!" Parrish’s gaze never faltered. "Or your best man. You choose. I will fight anyone you decide to put against me."

“I see.” The smaller Chieftain paused for a moment, thinking.

He turned and briefly regarded his own loyal men. Clearly each was ready and willing to fight the tall one. To the death if necessary. After all, what a great trophy the head of a Chieftain would make.

"Any?" Shimon asked slowly. “Any of my men?"

“Any of your men.” repeated Parrish. And that was his mistake.

Shimon nodded. He saw a chance to guarantee victory against the tall one and secure the goods desperately needed by his people.

“Then I choose these three." He opened his arms to indicate the warriors behind him.

There was a stifled gasp from the holy man behind the Danebury group.

Before Parrish could answer Klud leapt furiously in front of his friend and hurled both an insult and a threat at the smaller Chieftain.

"A trick!" he cried. "He offers you an honourable death and you try to trick him. For that I will kill you myself." His hand was already at his war club and in response the three opposing warriors leapt to defend their own leader.

Shimon showed his metal by not flinching at all and Parrish had to admit that he was impressed. By the man's savvy as much as his nerve. He knew he had underestimated the opposition and in war that could be a costly, even fatal mistake.

"STOP!" he barked and the power of his voice was such that everyone froze.

Shimon's glance darted to the tall man and there was an undeniably smug look on his face.

"You are a clever Chieftain." Parrish offered a brief complementary nod.

"A trick it may be but I will stand by my word. I accept your terms."

There were nods of approval from the three challengers, one of satisfaction and the acknowledgment of a man of honour from Shimon, but cries of dismay from both Klud and Tomps. Those behind Chieftain Shimon began to draw their weapons and spread out a little to give themselves room.

At that moment the Danebury holy man stepped around from behind Parrish and raised his hands in a signal to stop. Respect for a holy one, whoever he represented, was universal and both groups were stopped again at the edge of battle.

“It is agreed, yes." stated the shaman. "But the fighting must wait. At least for a short while."

"What!?" quizzed warriors on both sides.

The two Chieftains stayed their men with waves of the hand and waited for the holy man's reasons. Both knew his words would carry weight.

“The great wise one himself watches from Dane-bre even as we speak. He and his followers have travelled from the temple of Dannu to meet with Parrish for they have a task for him to do this very night. Your quarrel will have to wait, at least until the morrow."

It was all Shimon would get as an explanation but he was satisfied. His respect for the holy ones was as great as the next mans, perhaps even more so, having to deal with them on occasion in his capacity as a Chieftain. He could wait one more day for both supplies and victory.

“So be it." he nodded. "At high of the sun tomorrow Parrish, you do battle with my men here. The prize is our right to take whatever we need from your village without fear of attack." He grinned confidently.

“So be it." repeated Parrish curtly.

“Do not worry tall man. We will see you safely into the arms of Dannu."

Parrish just scoffed and without another word spun on his heel and strode swiftly away.

Klud and Tomps fell in alongside him while the holy man kept a discrete pace or so behind as they made their way back to Danebury.

"Three!" exclaimed Tomps. "You are the best, my Chieftain, but three. And they looked like good men."

"Tomps is right." said Klud. "They are too many my friend,

even for you. I say that the moment battle is joined we should step forward too and kill them all where they stand. Then all our warriors will attack in force and slaughter the rest of his people like lambs."

Parrish waved them both to silence.

“I do not think so. They would not die so easily as you think and many would be killed on both sides for no purpose. Even if I am killed it would only be one death instead of many, but it is not my intention to die tomorrow. Besides," he added. "I gave my word."

“I still do not like it." said Tomps, not quite under his breath.

"Nor I." agreed Klud loudly. "You will need to be at your very best tomorrow for any chance of victory and there is still the matter of what the holy ones have planned for you this coming night."

"There is wiseness in what you say Klud." interrupted their holy man, who had been listening to the conversation in silence. "But what the wise one needs done is more important even than what might happen tomorrow. I cannot say more but believe me when I tell you all that it is so."

Klud just grunted a begrudging acknowledgment and the little group lapsed into a subdued silence. They approached the main gate under the expectant gaze of the village before entering the hillfort to tell its astounded people of the arrangement for the following day.

6

Juli's face was clouded with worry as she checked her husband over before they both set off towards the great shrine hut. Although she would not say, she could not console herself over her husband's apparent madness at agreeing to take on three fit and determined warriors in single combat. And in these Neolithic times fighting warriors in combat always meant to the death. True, she had witnessed Parrish kill three men at once before, but one man had been totally mad and the other two unsuspecting and unprepared. This time though, his opponents would be keen, ready and looked very, very able.

She checked once more that her husband's combat jacket, that strangely coloured coat that he had worn the day he first walked out 'of Dannu's land, was as neat as possible. If he was actually going to be presented to Dannu herself Juli would wish him to be as fine and neat as she could manage without appearing to be fussing over him. Her official reason was that he should look his best for a religious occasion but there was also vanity there. It was understandable. She was very proud of her tall husband, his deeds and the admiring way everyone else looked at him and respected him. Loved him.

Be prepared to travel light, the wise one had said, so Parrish had put some strips of dried jerky in one pocket and his best flint dagger in another. There would be no need for real knives, he considered, for there would be no real journey, and so he fully intended to leave his MOD survival knife here at home. But he still put on his good buckskins and wore his now rather battered combat boots.

“Whatever the holy ones ask you to do," Juli said quietly, only daring in private to attempt to offer her husband some advice. “Try not to exert yourself too much. Save your strength for tomorrow."

To her surprise he laughed and took her into his arms.

“Do not worry." he said.” I am sure they too wish me success in the morning and so would not work me too hard tonight.”

He kissed her tenderly and looked deep into her blue eyes. He could see that a flood of tears seemed only a few tight blinks away.

"I ... I am sorry." she blurted, turning her face away and burying it into his chest in an attempt to hide her feelings from her husband. Parrish thought it an enchanting gesture.

"Do not worry." he said gently, cupping the back of her head in one hand and stroking her long dark hair. “Everything will happen as it should. Trust me."

She looked up then and he smiled down at her. He received a weak smile in return and in an attempt to cheer her more opened his mouth to speak again. The words remained unsaid as Klud called loudly from outside.

“My Chieftain. The moon is almost at its height. They are ready for you now."

Parrish scanned his house quickly, eyes settling on the little swathed bundle that was his son.

“Come on then." He put one arm reassuringly around his wife’s shoulders. “Chris will be all right here. He sleeps soundly and Dannu watches over him."

Juli believed him utterly and, with a smile and a nod went with him to the door before shucking out of his embrace to follow him out of their cabin, one step behind as a dutiful wife should.

The moon was indeed high and bright in its fullness as it lit the trio's pathway down towards the shrine hut. Looking away from the source of the soft light Parrish realized that most of the rest of the sky was cloudy and it was as if the moon was almost forcibly showing itself, pushing through the cloud cover to make sure it could be seen. As they approached the shrine hut Klud stopped his friend and offered out one hand. Clutched in it was a fine, brand new flint dagger.

"You may be in need of a weapon on your journey." he said gravely. Parrish nodded and, with a secret smile, dropped the dagger into his pocket where it nestled against the first one.

Klud led the way through, holding back the door blanket for both the Chieftain and his wife, and they all entered the shrine hut.

To Parrish's surprise he saw that the hut was full of villagers. He had expected the holy ones but not the entire adult populous of Danebury. They were congregated near the entrance, on the far side of the big central fire to the great statue. They parted to let him through and, while Klud and Juli remained with the others, he walked on towards where the old wise one waited in silence beneath the towering, bulbous form of the Earth Goddess.

The grey haired man welcomed him with open arms and summoned him forward until they both stood right beneath the statue.

"Why are my people here?" the tall man asked quietly. "I thought this would be a ceremony only for Dannu's servants."

"We are all Dannu's servants." replied the old sage. "Their part in this may be small but to them it is important and any help now is to be welcomed. Also, you are their Chieftain and it is right that they should try to be of help to you."

Parrish could not disagree. He turned to look at his people, still all gathered behind the central fire but now spread out across the back of the hut. He smiled and there were several nods of acknowledgment.

"How can they help?"

"When the chanting starts." explained the wise one. "At that time they have all been told to think as hard as they can about the goodness of the Earth Goddess. It may be a small token in this great event but the more who try to summon her, the better the chance of your journey. When the moon reaches its height, we must all be ready. You must be ready."

I am ready now." said Parrish. "And so are all my people. What more could you ask?"

"You do not understand, my tall friend." The grey haired man's rustly voice became suddenly quiet. " *Everyone* is ready. Not just here at Dane-bre. When we set off on our journey here messengers were also sent to all the other villages of the south lands. Every holy man and every villager that could be gathered up will right now be before their shrines and ready to call Dannu. We holy men here, picked because of our openness to her, are to gather up all that calling and bring it here to help you on your journey."

Parrish was simply dumbfounded. What could he say? He didn't understand the 'gathering up' bit but knew a truly gargantuan effort of organization and timing must have gone into making everything the old man had said happen. Something he knew would be no mean feat with twentieth century communications and was therefore totally astounding in these Neolithic times.

And yet for all that work, what did he honestly hope to achieve by it?

Before Parrish could form a reply the old man steered him to a position directly facing the statue of Dannu.

"You must go home to help her." he said quietly, so quietly that no one else heard, but with such reverence that Parrish knew it was no idle remark.

Then, in a louder voice said. "Look only up at Dannu and pay great attention to the light."

It was then that Parrish became aware of the subtle, soft, dancing light that played across the smooth roundness of the stonework. Cleverly placed tallow lamps both to the sides and suspended from above gave the effect of viewing the effigy through a sort of shimmer. Like a hovering heat haze.

The holy men gathered quickly on either side of him and began humming, a prelude to one of their chants. The tall man was aware of the people of Danebury at his back, watching in silence and with intense curiosity. He wanted to turn and offer them a confident smile but suddenly found it almost impossible to pull his eyes from the statue.

One last holy man, who had been waiting patiently outside observing the slow passage of the moon, appeared at the wise one's side and said simply.

“It is time."

The old man raised his hands high as a start signal. Most of the candles beyond those around the statue were extinguished, dropping all but the statue area of the hut into a soft half-light, and as one the holy men began a soft chant.

Parrish continued to stare up at the image of Dannu as the chanting around him began to grow louder and more invasive.

It crept unstoppably inside his head and oddly seemed somehow more audible than it should, as if it were being made by many more that the few who surrounded him. The dancing light before him began to increase in brightness, slowly at first but all the time gathering with ever more intensity.

The chanting filled his head and the light began to sting his eyes but he could not look away. Then, to his surprise, he felt them. Felt them all.

Holy men he had never met and people from villages he had never seen. All gathering around him and wishing him on with all their might. The holy ones on both sides, concentrating in a way they had not done before, also felt the sudden, awe inspiring surge as it flooded through them. Parrish could feel these privileged few gathering up all the goodwill and strong intent, focusing it, and pushing against him with it. Pushing him from all sides, as if trying to somehow compress him into a smaller space within himself. The pushing built up into a pressure and it seemed the only release from it was through Dannu. Up towards Dannu. Parrish stared through the now blinding whiteness as the chanting and pressure of the hundreds of minds wished him, no, willed him on.

And then the whiteness was everywhere. He could not see through the dazzle yet neither could he close his eyes. But he had a greater concern for now the pressure on him was becoming heavy. Unbearable.

The holy men around him, eyes shut and beads of perspiration glistening on their faces, continued to chant in unison. It took great effort to channel the power at the focal point in front of them but they struggled on for they had almost reached their goal in this event that had never before been done. Concentration and effort was everything now.

The villagers of Danebury were trying their hardest too and every little helped but, with no training and little real knowledge of what was being attempted before them, could do no more. Then, drawn to their beloved Chieftain as if mentally picked up and carried towards him by the will of countless, unseen others, each and every one of them looked up at the very moment Parrish cried out in sudden pain. They witnessed him jerked almost bodily up onto the balls of his feet, unnaturally balanced there as every muscle in his body went into spasm then locked rigid.

Every jaw hung slack with amazement as a faintly blue, shimmering glow like Saint Elmo's fire began to materialize along the edges of his body and within moments completely swathed the tall man from head to toe. The air immediately around him seemed somehow to get thicker, almost blurring what could be seen directly behind him, while the air in the rest of the great hut became unnaturally still and heavy like the lull before a summer storm.

Parrish was aware on none of this. In his paroxysm of pain and blinding light he saw only a vision, blurred in outline by the white dazzle. A vision of a woman. She was quite a way off in front of him but he saw the smile of recognition there. Then, in a slow, unhurried way she beckoned him towards her.

The people of Danebury saw their Chieftain, swathed in the mysterious blue glow, try with one great effort to lift himself even higher, as if reaching for something no one else could see, even though his arms were locked rigidly by his sides.

For a moment he hung, poised forward in his impossible tip-toe position, and those with a quick eye saw the air about him momentarily swirl, like an eddy in a stream.

Then there was a soft, white flash that had no sound and the Chieftain of Dane-bre simply blinked out of existence, vanished from sight right before the astounded eyes of the people he loved.

A split second later a single, tremendous clap of thunder rent the air outside, shaking the shrine hut to its foundations yet unable to shake those inside, rigidly aghast with shock and amazement.

1998

7

Parrish awoke slowly and found himself looking up into the leafy, spreading canopy of a huge beech tree. He was laying on his back, immediately aware of rich grass beneath him. After blinking a few times he did the natural thing and sat quickly upright. His senses, having taken a battering from a totally unnatural experience, understandably rebelled against their mistreatment. His semi-circulars swirled.

“Oh ... shit!" he exclaimed and put his hands to the ground to steady himself, screwing his eyes tight shut as stars exploded in his vision. What the hell happened? He took deep breaths and allowed himself some time for his spinning brain to come back onto an even keel.

It was then that he recalled the holy ones, the chanting, the light. Then ... nothing.

Slowly opening his eyes again revealed more normal vision and the previous swirling rapidly receded to a dull throb at the base of his brain. Somehow he knew that would soon go too, a vague memory perhaps that he had experienced such a thing once before. Climbing slowly to his feet he absent mindedly massaged the back of his aching neck and took a slow look around.

The place he found himself in was vaguely familiar, that was clear in an instant, but just exactly where from he could not immediately recall. And the air. It didn't have that sweet, clear quality that he had known. It tasted sort of old. Grubby. The sky was bright enough though with fluffy, summery clouds and it was pleasantly warm. Instinctively Parrish surveyed the sky with a now practiced eye and gasped at what he saw there.

High up in the blue, leaving a long, thin, white vapour trail behind it, was the silvery shape of a commercial jet liner.

“My God!" He gasped. "Surely it can't be?"

He looked hurriedly about him once more and a horrific realization of exactly where he was dawned. In a sudden panic he tried to flee from the terrible revelation, running down the slope towards where he knew the entrance was, passing between shrubs, bushes and several more well established trees. He didn't get too far before he found himself on a grassy pathway then came across an angled information board, tilted up at knee height to make it easily readable. The starkness of this man-made object against the natural backdrop pulled him to a sharp stop.

Not noticing that he was looking at printed English, Parrish quickly read the legend upon it.

A RELIGIOUS FOCUS

Here we are close to the center of the hillfort, where diggers found four unusual rectangular buildings. These were in line with the main gate, from where they appeared to be on the top of the hill. They may have been shrines for the Iron Aged folk, who firmly believed in magic powers. The people of Danebury and the surrounding farmsteads may have gathered here to listen to recitals of their Celtic myths and to watch their priests perform ritual sacrifices.

“Oh, really." said Parrish sarcastically under his breath before realizing the enormity of the sign’s significance.

He looked up at what he knew was the remains of his village. The five thousand five hundred year old remains of his village!. Everyone and everything gone. Gone forever. It choked him. Nothing now but bare patches of grassland, trees, shrubs and overgrown ditches that had not been maintained in over two thousand years, not since the hillforts fall at the hands of the Romans.

What about my wife, baby, friends? My village? The thoughts screamed shrilly inside his head. All gone and lost in the mists of time. Parrish let out a terrible cry and fell to his knees, fists clenched tight in front of his face.

“You sent me on a journey all right, you bastards." his voice somewhere between a venomous hiss and a sob. Hate welled up, boiling hot inside him, but there was no way or no one to vent it on and after a while common sense once more took control, telling him in an almost coldly detached way that whatever had happened had obviously not been done without thought and reason.

This can't be the end of it matey, he told himself, trying to reason some way out of this insanity. If this is not some horrible dream and I really have been sent forward, it must surely be possible for them to take me back? Isn't it? The last words held more than a hint of desperation.

It seemed really unlikely, he knew deep in his heart, but it was the only straw of hope he had to grasp at. And he grasped it with both hands.

Yes. It was possible. Had to be possible. But when and how?

Parrish sat on the ground and burned up several silent minutes in a determined attempt to get his head together.

Think now, think. He beat his thigh with a clenched fist as if to prove to himself that it was all real, this sudden nightmare. He could just sit there and wait for something to happen. Like maybe the holy ones magically reappearing and whisking him back but he had no idea how they might manage that, let alone just how or when. If at all.

No. Assuming he wasn't experiencing some kind of incredible hallucination and he really *had* been sent on this journey, then it had been done for a reason. He was on a mission.

“OK. I'll play the game.” he finally said loudly, to no one at all. “If I do what has been asked of me, then can I go home?"

There was of course no answer to his question.

Parrish nodded in acknowledgment anyway, after all what option did he have, then tried to push all the fears to the back of his mind and apply himself to the task ahead. Whatever that task might be. Anything to stop him thinking about the distinct possibility of never seeing his family, friends and village again. He didn't think he could bear that.

Then can I go home, he repeated in his mind. Go home. That was what the old wise one had said. You must go home to help her.

In this twentieth century, and he knew it had to be that if there were aircraft about, 'home' was his home town of

Southampton.

Parrish rose slowly to his feet, took one last, painful look at the derelict shell of what had once been the village of Danebre, his home, then with a great effort turned his back on it all and walked slowly down the slope towards the lower ground.

Just outside the gated entrance stood a grubby, off white coloured concrete bollard that he knew was one of the old trig points. Once used by cartographers to map out the land, these old trigonometrical points were now redundant relics, superseded by the high technology of satellites. He felt a sudden affinity with it and couldn't resist giving it a hesitant pat as he passed by. Yep, solid concrete all right.

Cresting the next low brow, he came to a sunken expanse of tarmac that was the visitor’s car park. So simple a thing and yet it seemed unreal to witness. Along with the fact that he did not now seem to know what was around a place he supposedly knew intimately, it somehow forced him to accept what he already really knew, drove home the point that the unthinkable truly had happened. On one hand he was filled with wonder for the incredible thing that had happened to him, yet on the other the painful logic of his mind was telling him that now those that had sent him on his journey were all dead and gone, five and a half thousand years in the past, he had surely travelled on a one way trip.

With a heavy heart he crossed the car park, negotiated the cattle grid at its entrance, marveling at the ringing sound of his boots against the metal tubing, then walked in steady, measured strides down the approach road to its junction with the road proper. Standing rather forlornly at its edge, he stared down at the white center line, somewhat at a loss as to what to do next.

Just then a sound came to his ears. One he recalled but couldn't initially identify.

The quiet roar of approaching tyres on tarmac.

From his left a car came into view, rapidly drawing nearer. In a short time it was with him, roared by at what he thought was incredible speed and rapidly disappeared from sight over the brow beyond. Parrish’s nose immediately screwed up at the foul odour of the exhaust fumes but otherwise he simply watched in dumb amazement.

Come on! He barked at himself. Get a grip. This is no way for a Chieftain to act. Home.

Parrish instinctively gauged his position from the sun, turned to his right and started to walk along the verge, heading south towards Southampton. As he walked he struggled towards some kind of acclimatization, attempting to gear his mind towards modern day thinking. It was very hard.

Crossing the road so that his back would be to any passing traffic heading in his direction, he continued on at an ambling pace, scanning the immediate area to catch sight of any more accurate proof of his position in time. Farm buildings, storage silos, the occasional road sign and power or telephone lines were his first observations.

The sound of another approaching vehicle made him turn and he saw a large box wagon closing. In true hitch-hiker fashion he thrust out a raised thumb and, to his surprise, the vehicle began to slow. An indicator flashed and the van passed him before pulling in to the side of the road.

Perhaps a Chieftain still has some sway, he thought rather conceitedly, even here.

Inside the cab the driver leaned across the bench seat and pushed open the passenger door. Parrish stepped into his view.

"Er ... thank you for stopping." was all he could think of to say.

“Fuck!" said the driver with real feeling, disappointment souring his heavy set features. "A bloody foreigner."

Parrish was momentarily startled to be addressed in English but quickly recovered his composure, realizing he'd been speaking in the now ancient tongue of his own people.

“No, no. Sorry. I'm English alright, it's just been a while since I've heard it spoken. I've ... ah ...I've been away." he added in a less than convincing tone.

The driver failed to notice and just nodded his head sagely, as if he knew everything.

“Been in a strange land for a while, eh?"

"Something like that."

“Well, jump in mate." The driver beckoned with one hand and Parrish followed the instruction and climbed up into the cab, barely having time to close the door behind him before the man ground the engine noisily into gear and pulled away with no more than a cursory glance into his rear view mirror.

“Africa I reckon." said the driver as he worked the engine aggressively up to a reasonable speed. "An' judging by your clobber I'd say you was ex- army. Probably went off on a wander after de-mob and liked it there."

" How could you tell?" asked Parrish in mock amazement.

"Not much gets past Dave Williams, that's me by the way. I spotted it right off when you spoke that foreign lingo back there. African I thought, and I was bang on, right?"

Parrish grinned widely at Dave who grinned right back, totally misunderstanding that it was not a smile of friendship but one of gratitude for being handed on a plate a ready-made cover story that could explain away his appearance to those that might question it.

“Right enough." agreed Parrish. "I left the Army and sort of went walkabout." He then realized he hadn't introduced himself properly.

“I am Chief ... er ... Parrish. My name's Parrish. Shaun."

“All right Shaun." came back Dave's loose but cheerful acknowledgment, before he carried right on with what he was about to say. "D'you know, when I first saw you I was in two minds whether to stop or not. At first glance you looked like one of them New Age travelers. You know, save the trees an' all that, but you're all right." he repeated. "Anyone who's served Queen an' country is welcome in my cab."

"Much obliged."

“Where you headed, Shaun?" Dave hauled on the big wheel before him, swinging the vehicle through a tight bend then on down a hill into Stockbridge.

“I hope to make it to Southampton."

"You're in luck mate!" exploded Dave with an even wider grin. "I'm going right into the docks there mi'self."

“Then I'm with the right man.” said Parrish.

His driver nodded enthusiastically and Parrish at last allowed a small grin to cross his face, knowing that while he was not the brightest of individuals, Dave came across as genuine enough in his helpful, cheerful manner.

Clearly the man was very pleased to have company for the rest of his trip because he immediately began to talk almost incessantly about a multitude of things that Parrish had no comprehension of. The latest results of football matches, the attributes of certain players including some with very foreign sounding names, television programs, and all the while finding time to ogle any female that happened to be nearby, be she walking or driving another vehicle.

Parrish just sat back and tried to take in all the sights and sounds of the twentieth century that surrounded and passed him by as he was carried through the Hampshire countryside at what seemed like breakneck speed. In reality the much abused engine of the box wagon rarely managed to push the vehicle in excess of forty five miles per hour.

All the while the occasional laddish, knowing laugh and nods in the right places seemed to keep Dave happy enough with his virtually one sided conversation, while Parrish kept a look out for some indication of a more exact time scale to his predicament.

The interior of the cab was cluttered, rather untidy and Parrish couldn't help wrinkling his nose at the multitude of generally unpleasant odours that filled it. Now he began to pay it more attention, letting Dave chatter away and charge relentlessly on down the road with his rather disconcertingly cavalier attitude to other, generally smaller, road users.

There was a much crumpled daily tabloid newspaper wedged between the base of the windscreen and the dashboard, directly above Dave's instrument panel. Parrish indicated it and although busy negotiation a junction, the driver stilt found time to snatch it up and toss it in his general direction, not once taking his eyes from the road ahead.

"Nice tits on her." he said with a leering grin.

Parrish plucked the paper deftly out of the air and spread it on his lap, not hearing the words as his attention became focused on the date beneath the papers title.

“Is this today’s?" he asked, trying hard to keep the shock out of his voice.

"Yeah."

May 4th, it stated in small but undeniable print. 1998!

"Shit!" he gasped.

"Yeah." repeated Dave." She is a big girl isn't she."

Parrish sat in silence again, eyes closed as he let this next shock wash over him.

After allowing a few moments to steady himself he re-focused on the newspaper and quickly riffled through the rest of it in an attempt to glean any further useful information, perhaps something concerning any major events that had happened since he had last been here, nearly a decade earlier. But there was nothing else he could find in the rather pointless rag and he eventually threw it contemptuously back onto the dashboard in front of him.

The Chieftain of Danebury finally sank back into his seat in the smelly cab, gazing in a rather dazed manner at all the traffic, roads, buildings and the huge numbers of people that passed by. It was the sheer number of people that took a little while to get used to. Parrish took full advantage of this rest time and attempted to gather his thoughts.

Dave continued to talk, still mostly concerned with football until, in a little over twenty minutes later by the small dashboard clock, they drove off the motorway spur and into the western edge of the city of Southampton.

The cranes and neatly stacked containers that crowded around the dock side were now clearly visible from the road and Dave steered the wagon to the curbside, pulling up directly alongside a signpost indicating next right into the docks.

"This is a far as you go, mate."

“Thanks." Parrish shot out his hand towards the trucker and Dave, although a little surprised by the gesture, manfully took it and they shook.

“Shit! That's one hell of a grip you've got there Shaun. Remind me not to meet you up an alley one dark night." He grinned at his little joke. "Anyway, thanks for the company and good luck. Oh, by the way." he added as Parrish jumped out onto the pavement. "If I was you, I'd take a bath, you know?"

He roared away, giving Parrish barely enough time to swing the door shut. The tall man stood slack jawed at the side of the road, amazed at the parting words.

He'd thought it was Dave who smelt bad!

8

Not exactly sure where he was going, Parrish just followed his nose and ambled at an easy pace through the western suburbs of the great city, making his way steadily towards its center.

While being permanently uncomfortable with the volume of humanity, the crowding, suffocating towering of the hard, solid buildings and the dirty taste of the fume filled air, he was at the same time beginning to feel more and more at ease with his old familiarity of the place. A place that he knew well and had once before, and it now seemed a lifetime ago, simply taken for granted.

Approaching the center of town he soon found himself surrounded with shops of every description and couldn't resist peering into each window as he passed, seeing the things on offer there now with a new eye and completely different perspective. All at once marveling at the easy access to the foods and other necessities of life, along with the myriad of appliances that made the living easy, and the toys that the people used to fill up their now ample spare time.

And yet with all this at their fingertips, with the new millennium and the twenty first century so close at hand for this great moderness of so called civilization, he knew the people who now lived often found their lives difficult. Sometimes almost unbearable.

Yet some things had not changed at all, from the time of his own people to the present day. These things had a certain inevitability about them. OK it appeared less obvious to the casual observer, someone without a different perspective to view things from but they were still there. Hidden by a thin veneer of respectability, so called equality and with the advent of feminism, it was still plain enough to Parrish that this was still a world where for the most part women were subservient to men.

He passed a sex shop and could tell even from the few, less offensive items displayed in the window, that most of them were for draping on, tying against or applying to women's bodies.

In the high street there was now an Anne Summers shop displaying all sorts of revealing clothing, not much more than carefully placed scraps of cloth really, for women to wear for the titillation and teasing of men with. It was a market almost wholly generated by men for men at the expense and often the exploitation of the female form.

Even so, a smile escaped from Parrish's lips as he gazed briefly at the merchandise on offer, realizing with a knowledge few others had that at the end of it all it was that same sexual power that women wielded against their men folk, using both their guile and their bodies to get what they really wanted, needed or desired, by apparently pandering to the base needs of men while their own reasoning's and drives ran much deeper. This was the true gift from Dannu to her daughters and, without realizing it, the men of the world were, in all matters that really mattered, being subtly led, directed or at least guided along the general path where the women wanted them to go. If their needs or desires were the same as those of their opposite sex, then the system worked all the better.

In a sudden flash of inspiration, the Chieftain of Danebury understood it all, and that there was a great truth in the saying 'Behind every good man there is a good woman.'

Parrish alone knew also that behind all good women was the greatest woman of all. Dannu.

He moved on, finding the pedestrian precinct area of the town center almost unbearably crowded even though it was mid afternoon and many people were at work. He also hated the squalor. Not the squalor that twentieth century folk associated with poor housing, poor prospects and the living conditions of slum areas but the general squalor of the place. The litter, carelessly discarded rubbish, the waste of materials and the uncaring attitude of the people to it all.

Instinctively he headed for greenery and found some relief from the pressure of the seething humanity in the grassy, tree lined haven of Palmerston Park. It was only a token acknowledgment to the natural world, with its cultured flower beds, manicured lawn areas, crisscrossing concrete footpaths and regimented tree lines but Parrish still smiled to see it and sank gratefully to the bare soil beside one of the paths to ponder the seriousness of what he hoped to do next. Or more exactly just where he should start.

While he was thinking, staring down without seeing at the ground before him, the loud caw of a carrion bird sounded from high above him. Hearing a sound he instantly recognized he looked up to locate its source, a huge black crow sitting on an outcropping branch from the tall lime tree that towered upward from the opposite side of the path.

At that very moment a young couple passed across Parrish's line of vision, momentarily obscuring his view of the bird. His piercing eyes instantly took in their closeness and comfortable intimacy.

A bond forming there, he thought.

His gaze momentarily captured theirs and, almost without thinking, the girl dipped a hand into her pocket and tossed a golden coin into his lap. The pair had barely broken stride as they passed and while Parrish gazed down in surprise at the coin he could hear clearly their receding voices.

“Why d'you do that?" asked the lad.

“I dunno." came the girls reply. “S'funny but I don't usually pay any attention to beggars. He just looked as if he could really use the money. P'raps he can get himself a coffee."

“Or make a call." said Parrish under his breath, picking the coin carefully out of his lap before rising easily to his feet.

Oblivious to what was happening far below, the big crow lifted out of the tree and flapped almost casually away, oblivious too of the loose salute aimed in his direction by the man in buckskin trousers now going off in search of a telephone booth with a directory in it.

There was a delay when Parrish found that modern phone boxes did not hold directories. One had to dial for directory enquiries but the soulless voice on the other end could give no number without an address and it was the address that Parrish needed more than the number. Thinking modern showed a solution to his problem and he made his way, with more purpose now, to the central public library.

Despite his odd appearance, or maybe even because of it, the librarian he asked for assistance from was more than happy to help him find the information he needed. Having enjoyed herself so much when she had been at both college and university the woman was glad to help a fellow struggling student, even if he was more unusually dressed than most others she'd seen, and had stupidly allowed his face and hands to be marked with that indelible India ink. The result of a rag week prank or the aftermath of some serious and wild party, she didn't wonder.

There were a large number of Dunn's in the phone book but only seventeen that had a Christian name beginning with the letter C. Fortunately this number was even further reduced by the inclusion of second Christian name initials. Those that had the correct second name numbered only five. Parrish just hoped that his friend was at least in the book or hadn't gone ex-directory.

Using one of the pay phones in the reception area of the building he slotted in his single one pound coin and punched in the first number.

It was too much to expect success first attempt and so he wasn't surprised when an old lady answered his call and politely said that she had never married.

The second number on his list produced a voice with a distinct Welsh twang.

Parrish watched his limited monetary reserve dwindling in sharp steps. The next call drank up more when he got through to some strange individual who took several expensive moments to decide that he wasn't sure if his name was Chris but did the caller want to buy a colour television? Parrish cut him off.

Only if he was quick with the next caller could he stretch to the fifth and final number, he knew.

He began to think his luck had run out when the fourth call rang for quite a while before he was put through to an answer machine. Just as he was about to urgently bang down the receiver the taped voice piped in.

"Sorry but Chris and Lorraine aren't in at the moment. If you leave ..." Parrish had heard enough and gently put the receiver back into its cradle.

The voice was instantly recognizable and he allowed himself a smile as he checked the address that corresponded with the fourth number. He raised one eyebrow.

"Hmm, Basset eh? Seems ol' Chris has gone up in the world, and attached too by the sound of it."

He returned the directory to the librarian, not even bothering to see if the telephone would surrender the small amount of change due him. It didn't anyway. Borrowing a pencil and scrap of paper he wrote down the address. It momentarily felt strange actually writing again after so long but his style appeared natural enough when he looked at it. Just as he remembered.

Winking his thanks at the helpful lady, which earned him the most charming smile in return, he left the library with determined strides. Parrish was going to call on an old friend.

It would most probably be a bit of a shock, he mused. Possibly for them both.

By the time Parrish arrived in Basset it was late in the afternoon, the sun now well on its way towards the horizon.

The house in question was situated quite a way off the main drag that led out of the north of the city. It was tucked away in a quiet, secluded spur off of a side road. Almost central among the row of a dozen large, detached houses in a cul-de-sac shaped like a half crescent moon, it and all the other buildings in the road faced across the tarmac, overlooking a thin swathe of woodland that separated the edge of the housing area from the open greenery of the municipal golf course.

It was easy enough to find number five and, rather than just barge straight in on the unknown, the Chieftain of Danebury moved across the road and into the tree line opposite. Finding himself a position that enabled observation of both the house and the rest of the street without being seen, at least by the casual observer, he did what he was expert at and settled down to watch and wait.

All was quiet in this peaceful corner of the metropolis,

making Parrish now feel more at ease than he had since his arrival. He chewed slowly on a few pieces of his now five thousand five hundred year old jerky as he watched, an almost automatic action in response to the gentle reminders from his empty stomach.

He considered the situation as he saw it while sitting in shaded silence. It was plain enough, he reasoned, that to afford the luxury of such fine houses the occupants would be white collar workers on very good incomes. Thus he felt certain that, no matter whatever else had happened, it was most likely his old friend was no longer a member of Her Majesties Armed Forces.

Sometime between half five and half six, although Parrish had no way at all of gauging the time even if he had wanted to, people began to return to their homes after a hard day at the office. They were totally unaware of the cool, all seeing gaze that watched in a coldly detached manner as they climbed from their big Volvo's or BMW's and went inside. Their big, expensive four wheeled status symbols held no sway as far as the Chieftain of Danebury wasconcerned.

The first person to arrive outside number five was a woman, driving a very smart looking red two seater sports car. The vehicle's make did not interest Parrish as his attention became focused on its driver. The garage door opened up automatically and she drove inside, collected a bulging leather briefcase from the passenger seat, walked out of the garage and operated a small box in her free hand that set the garage door in motion again. By the time it had fully closed she was at the front door and fishing inside her bag for the key. Even though he watched from some sixty yards away, Parrish could see that she was an attractive modern woman. Her bearing and the well cut clothes she wore also indicated a woman of some substance, at least as far as money went. Did that also mean one of intelligence and drive or just the product of a silver spoon upbringing?

If this was the Lorraine mentioned on the answer phone tape, Clive Dunn might have done all right for himself. Parrish's thought suddenly brought back the memory of his own wife and it pained him deeply to think of Juli and just how much he missed her.

Moments later lights began to come on in the house, a waste

of energy thought Parrish, considering that it was still daylight, and occasionally he caught glimpses of the woman passing before one window. apparently making herself a drink in the kitchen. The sudden thought of the rich aroma of fresh coffee brought a little bit of cheer back.

It was a while later, although the sun was still a few hours from setting, when a second car pulled up in front of number five. This vehicle was a more standard looking Ford and showed early signs of being attacked by the weather. The smart car was already in the garage so this one no doubt stayed outside.

Much more a workhorse than a toy.

A man of similar build to Parrish climbed out and headed towards the house. He was a bit heavier set, had fair hair and was slightly taller. To the expert eye there was also the unmistakably military stamp on him too, the way he stood and the precise measure of his stride.

"Chris." breathed Parrish with a smile and watched intently as his old friend entered the building. It had only been a brief glimpse but it was enough. Satisfaction settled on Parrish like a warm cloak and he relaxed considerably now, leaning back as he decided to watch until darkness came before approaching.

This decision to wait was made because there was no way to predict just how a man would react when confronted with a ghost from the past. At least Parrish was pretty certain his friend wouldn't just faint clean away at the sight of him but although he knew the man's resolve was strong, he hoped the shock wouldn't overpower him and inadvertently cause a big scene on the doorstep that could be witnessed by all and sundry. Parrish had no wish to announce his arrival to the authorities if he could help it. Was it just the way of a modest and successful Chieftain that he tried where possible to keep a relatively low profile, or was there some deeper, inner voice which told him that keeping anonymous would ultimately be to his benefit?

The evening drew on, dusk came and went and night began to settle its black and all enveloping blanket across the land, the city and the little half crescent of houses that were still the object of Parrish's observations. Street lights and the odd illumination or two from the houses tried to hold back the darkness but it was a futile gesture. In contrast Parrish welcomed the coming of the night. It was safe and protective. You were hidden from the eyes of an enemy. It was the hunter's friend too, hiding him from his prey yet amplifying the sounds and smells of the land and the creatures on it. A good man who knew the lore of the forest could move through it in confidence, almost as quickly during the night as in the day. Only the weak minded or those in fear through ignorance were afraid of the night. The land of the Earth Goddess spent half its time in the darkness and to one with an open mind, a sound knowledge and self- assurance it was as beautiful when cloaked in stars and moonlight as it was bathed by the golden, warming rays of the sun.

It was time.

Parrish moved silently out of the trees and across the road, not being deliberately silent or stalking in his movement but still producing the same effect. It was now just the way of the man. He stepped up to the door, took a deep breath and boldly pressed the doorbell. After a few moments the hall light came on and there was movement behind the frosted panes. Almost abruptly the door swung inwards and Parrish came face to face with his past.

9

He looks definitely older, was Parrish's first thought.

"Yes?" Chris Dunn frowned at the mysterious, bearded, scruffy looking individual who stood before him.

"Clive, don't tell me you don't remember your old mucker?" said Parrish softly with a grin.

Chris was finding it hard to place the face of this person who very obviously knew him. Yet somehow in the back of his mind the recognition bell was ringing. It *was* familiar and no one he knew had called him 'Clive' in a long time.

Then it all came together. And although he knew it couldn't be, that voice was unmistakable.

The colour drained from the twentieth century man's face and there was a strained pause before he could bring himself to speak the single word.

"Parrish?" he gasped, his voice barely audible.

"Got it in one." Came the familiar, cheery reply, a fully fledged smile now on the bearded face.

"Jesus Christ!" Then again. "Jesus FUCKING Christ!" Chris rocked back on his heels as if he had been physically struck. His jaw gaped and for a few moments no more words would come.

All things considered, Parrish thought his friend was taking it rather well.

"Aren't you going to invite me in then?" he asked casually.

"But ... but, fuck me Shaun, your dead!"

"I don't think so. I'd still like to come in though."

Chris stepped dumbly aside and Parrish moved into the hall, closing the door quietly behind him while all the time his motionless friend stared on in amazement.

Now they had more privacy Parrish turned to face Chris and said in a gently voice.

“It's me mate, it really is me." He put a reassuring hand on his friend’s shoulder.

It seemed to be the touch that did it, a real, solid, flesh and bone touch. Although Chris still found it a massive shock, an unbelievable thing that stunned him to the core, there was now no denying that the man with him was his dead friend. Dead and buried years before, and still sadly missed.

"I can't believe it. I ...”

"It's OK. Just take your time." He saw his friend attempting to absorb the shock and trying to bounce back. This was the Clive he remembered so well.

“But ... but ... how?"

Before Parrish could reply a woman's voice called from inside the house.

"Who is it?"

Chris's head momentarily flicked back and forth. Everything was happening a bit fast for him.

“Ahh ... it's .. er .. it's an old Army pal of mine." he called back, the shock still evident in his voice. "Turned up a bit unexpected. I'll say.” he added under his breath. "I'll ... come on in Shaun." he indicated towards the lounge door, exhaling forcibly. "Fuck me, I need a drink."

Forgetting his manners, perhaps understandably, he led the way into the spacious room and want straight to the drinks cabinet leaving Parrish standing just inside the doorway.

Chris's wife watched disapprovingly as her husband poured himself a very stiff whiskey, before turning her gaze towards the stranger in her house. There was a fleeting moment deep within her when she'd instantly known he was there, even before she set eyes on him. She turned in her seat and found a strange man in her home, standing quietly, just watching. Without understanding she was briefly aware of a great presence. An aura. As if she were meeting someone of true substance.

But this was instinctive and not only not understood by the twentieth century but also not listened to. Here and now image and appearance was everything and the fleeting sense of the nearness of greatness was gone, smothered by the teachings of centuries of materialism, the pursuit of wealth and the class system. Without her deeply submerged natural instinct to guide her, all she finally saw was a scruffy, bearded man with long, unkempt hair wearing a very battered camouflage jacket, well worn, cheaply made leather trousers and very scuffed boots standing in her immaculately clean and neatly kept lounge.

“Lorraine, this is Shaun. Shaun Parrish." Chris gestured with his now empty whiskey glass. "A friend I haven't seen in ... well, about ten years actually." It was plain by the look on his face that he was still having trouble grasping it, shaking his head in disbelief at his own words. The gesture was lost on his wife and she rose to her feet, nose turned up in disgust.

“How long is he staying?" she snapped.

The hostility was plain and Parrish raised his hands in surrender.

“I'll go." he said apologetically. "I just wanted to say hello to an old friend. Sorry to have bothered you.”

“No ... no.” Chris moved smartly to his wife’s side. "Jesus." he hissed at her. "He's a guest in our home. I don't talk to your friends like that."

“My friends don't look like that.” she replied coldly, nodding towards Parrish.

"Yes," Parrish laughed another apology, looking briefly down at himself. "I suppose I could do bit a bit of a clean up, but you wouldn't believe the hard time I've had recently. All I've got right now is what I'm standing up in"

Chris started ushering his wife towards the kitchen, a gesture Parrish could see she really disliked.

“Put the kettle on love, please. I'll sort Shaun out a change of kit while he has a wash and brush up, and we'll start again, eh?"

Lorraine scoffed but nodded, ignored Parrish completely and went out into the kitchen. Almost immediately the sounds of crockery and cutlery could be heard being banged forcibly down onto work surfaces.

Chris pushed Parrish back out into the hallway then led him upstairs towards the bathroom.

“Sorry about that," he said. "but she kind of likes things all neat and tidy."

"That's OK mate." Parrish laughed. "I suppose I do look like shit."

"Yes but never mind that. How come you're here? Where the fuck have you been? What happened?"

"All in good time Chris, all in good time. First things first. Time for a dobie down."

"Right." For the first time a grin came to Chris Dunn's face as he recognized the old, solid, sensible way of things that was most definitely Shaun Parrish. And yet he had already noticed that there was now somehow more to his friend than he remembered. Something he couldn't put his finger on but was definitely there. Ignoring his shabby condition, there was no physical change that he could see but it was as if the man were somehow bigger, greater. Somehow just *more.*

He waved his friend into the bathroom and quickly collected some clothes from a bedroom before returning.

Parrish just seemed to be standing in silence in the middle of the bathroom. Anyone would think he hadn't seen a bath, shower or sink in ages.

"Shower there." he pointed, before handing his friend the pile of clothes. "Sweatshirt, trainers, pair of jeans." He slapped the top of the bundle in Parrish's arms. "Soap and towels. Spare razor in the cabinet."

Parrish, quickly recovering his composure, tugged at his familiar face growth.

"Beard off?" he asked light heartedly.

"Beard off." grinned back Chris and Parrish smiled at the first hint of his friends usually good humoured self. This was more like he remembered. He knew he could depend on Chris bouncing rapidly back. A good man when it came to riding the hard knocks of life. He'd known another good friend, long ago now, who also could do that.

A short while later Parrish appeared for a second time in the doorway of the lounge. Chris simply nodded an acknowledgment, another tumbler of whiskey in his fist.

Lorraine turned at the nod, not having heard her husband's friend enter. She'd never known someone who moved so quietly. The sight that met her eyes this time was much more pleasing and Parrish felt the almost immediate change in attitude towards him. Still disapproving, but not openly hostile.

He understood he was more acceptable to the twentieth century now, scrubbed clean as it were, and rubbed his bare chin, realizing he missed the growth more than he thought he would.

Lorraine now saw, instead of the previous apparition of a grubby tramp, a very well built man who seemed to fill the doorway even though she didn't consider him particularly large or over muscular. But his tremendous fitness was obvious even to the untrained eye. Although it still disgusted her to see the roughly drawn, somehow thuggish tattoo's around his neck and on his cheek, she now saw too the firm features and strong, if somewhat hard looking eyes.

His formerly long and unkempt hair was now glistening wet and pulled back, secured just above the nape of his neck into a short ponytail. Still not someone she would introduce to her well to do friends who, if the truth were known only accepted her husband under sufferance, she found Parrish much more toher liking. A working class man with a strong back and coarse hands but certainly some potential, she thought. The proverbial rough diamond.

"C'mon in mate." Chris beckoned warmly. "No need to stand on ceremony. Cuppa tea?"

“Yes." Lorraine was now the dutiful wife. "Please sit. One lump or two?"

Chris eyed his wife curiously for a moment as Parrish moved to the seat indicated and duly sat. He'd expected a harder time that this trying to convince his wife of his odd friends value.

"No sugar please but tea would be lovely."

Parrish smiled gratefully at her but had caught Chris's puzzled glance. It was becoming more and more obvious, even this soon after meeting the pair, that his old friend was in over his head as far as this woman was concerned.

For himself Parrish was not overly enamoured with Lorraine as a person. Although she obviously came from an upper class background and Chris seemed to be the working class boy come good, he thought that his friend could have done better as regards a wife. This was a marriage destined not to go the distance.

As if to confirm his thoughts Lorraine, although seeming to be all charm, suddenly cut them both off, eager it appeared, to be out of the way when two rough boys were about to get down to vulgar chat and reminiscing about their gutter past life. As she knew they soon would.

“There you are Mister Parrish." She elegantly handed him a bone china cup and saucer.

Parrish just as gracefully accepted the beverage but then shattered the illusion of refinement as he slurped it noisily to gain the maximum taste in appreciation of a drink he loved and had not savoured in a long time. And it did not disappoint, for naturally Lorraine only used the finest teas.

“Ahh .. that tastes *so* good." He smiled at his hostess, the look of distaste on her face not vanishing quite quickly enough to go unnoticed. “And please call me Shaun. Or just Parrish. My friends call me Parrish."

“Well, *Mister* Parrish." she replied, emphasizing the mister so the man new just where he stood.” I'm glad you like it but now, if you'll forgive me, I must go to bed. Big meeting in the morning."

With that she rose to her feet, gave no more than a cursory nod to her husband, then left the room with only a final pause in the doorway for effect.

And yet she made cunning use of that pause to take one last look at the stranger in her home. Despite her holier-than-thou attitude towards him as someone of a lower class or order, there was a strange attraction in him too. She couldn't say quite why or how but something touched her inner being, threatening to draw her towards him. She pushed the feeling back down and left the pair in the hard glow of the electric lighting, going upstairs to bed.

Parrish was unaware of the animal magnetism he projected towards the woman as Chris, who now sat opposite him in the chair his wife had just vacated, leaned forwards, cupped the now empty glass in his hands and spoke softly.

“Don't take it to heart mate, she'll come round. It often takes a while for her to accept my friends."

“And just how many has she accepted so far?"

"Er ... never mind that now. Let's talk about you. Tell me what the fuck happened to you? Where have you been? Why didn't you contact anyone? Everyone thinks you're dead! I mean, Christ, I even went to your funeral!"

"And that's the way it's got to stay, mate. No one must know I'm still about. Not a soul."

"But ..."

“No one." Parrish gave his friend a hard stare. "I want your word on it Chris. You're not to mention me at all. And I mean to anyone."

“I don't understand. Why ... "

"I have my reasons and that's all I'll say. But I want your word." There was a pause as a gamut of confused expressions crossed Chris Dunn's face but finally he nodded.

“You have it."

Parrish nodded too, satisfied that it would be enough. He felt sure Chris hadn't changed so much in ten years that the man had lost his integrity.

“Am I staying here tonight?" he said, changing the subject abruptly.

"The spare bedroom is yours, for as long as you want."

“Bet Lorraine won't be too happy about that." No wonder she didn't say good night to him, Parrish thought. She knew what was coming.

“Like I said, she'll come round." Chris dismissed the attempted change in direction. "Now tell me. What happened after you disappeared on Salisbury Plain that day?"

So Parrish told him.

But not everything, which was just as well because he could tell by the badly disguised look on his friends face that Chris didn't really believe much of the strange tale. Who could blame him? There was no real proof of it all even though the older man could not explain away the bones and the burial he'd attended some two years earlier. Yet that did not concern Parrish, who did not care either way about proving himself to anyone. He was Chieftain of Danebury and a man who spoke true. If others chose not to believe him then that was their affair.

So Parrish spoke in general terms of his arrival in Neolithic England, the discovery of Danebury and how he came to be one of the villagers who lived there. He did not mention that he was Chieftain or that there was a Goddess who watched over his people. The Goddess of an ancient, Pagan religion, who had personally sent him across time to do her bidding. When he looked at it like that he could scarce believe it himself.

Occasionally Chris would nod or ask the odd question, these gestures interspersed with a softly spoken 'fantastic' or 'amazing', but mostly he let his friend continue uninterrupted. He could tell by the man's gestures, expressions and just by knowing the man, that even if it were a total pack of lies, Parrish believed in it completely. And that was enough for Chris. He would keep to his vow of silence and let his friend play out his fantasy.

All the while the night wore on and as the pair talked they brewed and consumed copious amounts of tea. It appeared to be something else that Parrish hadn't seen in ages. And as the conversation turned the traveler too learned a few things about what had happened in the twentieth century during his absence.

Parrish was right in his original assumption. Chris had indeed left the Army, then worked through a stream of dead end jobs until becoming shop floor manager at an international company manufacturing high class clothing. The daughter of one of the company directors, high up in the firm herself as one of its materials purchasers, had spied this good looking, fit and athletically built individual making no small name for himself at shop level with his organizational skills at the Southampton factory. She made some discrete enquiries. Soon they were going out together and, against everyone's expectations, they were married eighteen months later. That was a little over a year ago. Even if Chris couldn't see it yet, it was plain to Parrish that the gloss had since gone from their union and Lorraine was getting bored with her conquest.

Chris clearly thought his wife beautiful, which indeed she was with her classical looks, firm breasts, long shapely legs and public school education.

Parrish thought that Lorraine, lovely as she was, simply saw her husband as a rather dashing, ex-Army action man. He also thought that she was a spoiled brat who was used to getting her own way, Chris was a gullible fool when it came to women and that neither person really loved the other. But one of Chris's finer qualities was that he was a loyal soul and in the end it would be she who left him, not the other way round. Sooner or later his old friend was going to get hurt.

Parrish wisely kept these thoughts to himself.

On a more personal level the Chieftain of Danebury was dismayed to be told that despite the best efforts of the Army and the emergency medical services, Professor James Barstow, inventor of the machine that had originally shot Parrish back in time, had sadly died as a result of the helicopter crash. The internal injuries he sustained were worse than first thought and he had gone into arrest during the flight out of the crash site. By the time the aircraft had landed in the hospital grounds it was too late. Chris wasn't certain but he felt pretty sure that because of this and the other deaths and disappearances of people involved in the incident, the MOD had closed the project run by Professor Barstow. No more steel balls were ever made.

It was with a heavy heart that Parrish now truly felt he would never return to his people, wife and son. The sadness settled heavy on his shoulders and Chris saw his friends suffering.

"Look." he said softly. "It's late. Why not get yourself some kip, eh? I've got an early start in the morning but we'll talk some more tomorrow night. Until then and for as long as you need, my house is your house, no matter what Lorraine says. OK?"

Parrish nodded slowly and the pair rose to their feet, both somehow knowing that the conversation and the evening had come to its end. Chris patted him on the back then led the way upstairs, stopping outside the spare bedroom.

"Things'll look brighter in the morning, mate." he said, trying to inject some lightness into the heavy silence.

"Yes, you're probably right." Parrish lied straight faced.

"Just get your head down and I'll see you tomorrow. G'night Shaun."

"Night." replied Parrish dully and went in.

Chris stood for a moment facing the door after it had closed, then shook his head and went back towards the room where his wife already lay.

"Parrish." he said softly to himself. "Fuck me. Parrish of all people. And the Stone Age no less. I dunno."

He shook his head once more, laughing softly through his nose, then fell silent as he crept into the bedroom, doing his best not to wake his wife.

10

Next morning, at seven thirty, Lorraine arrived outside the spare bedroom, a no nonsense figure in her staid grey suit and crisp white blouse. She listened briefly but could hear no sound and after a few moments rapped her knuckles firmly against the woodwork.

"Breakfast, Mister Parrish. Do you want any?"

There was no reply, even after a second, louder knock.

Without hesitation she tested the handle and, finding the door unlocked, pushed it wide. Even though considering herself well within her rights in her own home to enter any room she chose, her boldness stopped short of actually barging straight in. She never needed to for she was surprised to see the bed empty. And unused. The duvet had been removed and used as a makeshift bed on the floor beside the real thing. She frowned, uncomprehending. Who on earth would prefer a hard floor to a soft mattress?

As if in answer to the unspoken question the doorbell chimed downstairs.

Descending swiftly and opening the door she found Parrish standing at the threshold. He just looked at her, no discernible expression on his face.

"Oh. You weren't in your room ..." she began.

"No."

"Where ...?"

"I just needed a bit of fresh air," He shrugged. "and to see the sun come up through the trees."

"But it's nearly summer." she gasped. "Sunrise must have

been at about six o'clock."

Earlier actually, thought Parrish although he didn't say. He just shrugged again and slipped deftly past her into the house.

"Er ... breakfast in the kitchen." was all she could think of to say. “Bacon and eggs?"

"That's fine." He flashed a charming smile at her. "Lead me to it."

Lorraine realized she was fighting a losing battle when she found herself not only settling this strange man at the breakfast bar but preparing the bacon and eggs for him too, even after he had offered to cook the food himself. She didn't understand him at all, or the effect he was having on her. And the man appeared to be not the least bit fazed or intimidated by her high handed attitude, her power, wealth or even her good looks. At first glance he appeared to be a plain old scruffy, down and out wastrel, but there was something else there too and whatever it was, she was finding it, well, almost attractive.

“I'm afraid I'll have to leave you to finish off alone.” She was also becoming apologetic. "I've a board meeting at ten. And Chris has already gone. Left at around seven this morning."

“I know." And it was true for Parrish had watched unseen from the trees as his friend had departed.

“Yes ... well .. er .. we ‘ll both be back about the same time tonight. Please make yourself at home.”

Parrish smiled at the look on her face as she spoke the words. He had no doubt she had been coerced into making the offer by Chris and that she desperately wanted to add 'and don't touch anything' to the statement.

“You won't even know I've been here." he said cheerily, ignoring the hot food placed before him and rising to his feet. "And allow me to see you to the door."

Lorraine was even more bemused now. Gentlemanly conduct too! This friend of Chris's was full of surprises.

She gathered up her briefcase and he escorted her politely out. He even stood in the drive and watched while she extracted her car from the garage, not returning to his breakfast until the vehicle had finally vanished from sight out of the crescent. It was a puzzled woman who drove off to her board meeting.

And that's how it was for the next two days. Everything was

all politeness and friendly gestures on the surface while hidden inside, silent struggles were going on.

Chris was glad enough to have his long lost friend as a guest but could not account for his long absence. Neither was he convinced by the man's tall tale about time travel and life in the distant past.

Lorraine was torn between the two feelings she had. One of wanting to be rid of her husband's coarse, ruffian friend with his thuggish tattoo's and apparently zero prospects, the other a growing attraction she was beginning to feel towards this same man who somehow appealed to the deeply repressed but slowly emerging animal instinct side of her. She of course could not put into words or explain this attraction but it was never-the-less there, and well she knew it.

Parrish was stuck firmly in the middle of everything and unable now to do anything but wait. Yet it was not the waiting itself that bothered him, for it had once been said of him that he could outwait a stone. It was the uncertainty.

Just what was he waiting for? All the inactivity seemed to achieve was to give him plenty of time to ponder on the life and loves he had left so far behind.

During the evenings, whenever any conversation did spring up between the three, it always eventually seemed somehow to come around to the Stone Age. All this did was make Parrish homesick, deeply disturbed Chris that his friend should be so pre-occupied with his fairy story, and bored Lorraine who had no interest what-so-ever in the recent past, let alone ancient history.

The one thing she had done, in an attempt to make the odd man a little more presentable, was to buy for him a number of different coloured, high quality close fitting polo necked shirts. She had to admit that they fitted him rather well and emphasized just how fit he was, but their prime intention was to cover the dreadful line and ring tattoos around his neck. Now that he wore them only the cross hatch and five large dots high up on his cheek and the lines on the back of one hand were visible. Still not ideal, but definitely much more acceptable.

Parrish was initially unhappy with the feel of the material tight against his skin but overlooked it, suddenly realizing that apart from his own battered clothes and the few Chris had supplied, he had no other garments. Also, to move freely about in these modern times one other thing that did not exist in the Neolithic age was needed.

Money.

When they were alone he spoke with Chris about it.

"I knew you'd get round to it eventually." his friend smiled. "In fact, I've been impressed that you waited this long." He dipped one hand into a pocket and produced a tightly rolled wad of bank notes. "We've got a joint account and Lorraine deals with all our money matters but I've kept a small stash of my own. Just in case of emergencies you understand."

Parrish nodded and returned the offered wink. Most soldiers kept a small poke tucked away somewhere for any unforeseen 'emergency', although it was usually just a reserve to fund the next big drinking binge. Chris handed him the cash.

“Five hundred quid." he said proudly. "But don't tell Lorraine. It's every penny of my own money Shaun, and you're more than welcome to it."

“Thanks.”

Parrish was not ashamed to ask for the money and knew Chris was not offended that he had asked. He needed it, Chris was willing to part with it and besides, they were old soldiers who had learned long ago to rely on one another. But it was more than that. They were friends.

And all the time the waiting continued.

It was surely a touch of irony that it was in fact Lorraine who eventually set the wheels in motion. And with such a small thing too. Who could have guessed where it would all lead to.

It was evening and the three were in the lounge. A silence had descended after the small talk petered out, as was happening on an ever more regular basis. Chris began to wonder what was on TV. Parrish stared with melancholy into the small, dancing flames of the coal effect gas fire, while Lorraine turned her attention to the latest edition of one of the clutch of papers she regularly had delivered. It happened to be The Hampshire Chronicle.

She absent mindedly folded out of sight an article about some disturbance or other at the British Museum in London, while both reducing the broadsheet newspaper in size to make it easier to handle and bringing to the fore a small piece which she then ringed in red pen. Her eyes turned toward Parrish.

“Here's something that might just interest you." She thrust the paper at him. "What with you being keen on the Stone Age."

Gracefully accepting it he quickly read the few column inches of article highlighted, not much more than a brief report really.

Lorraine explained it in brief terms too for her husband, who had raised an eyebrow.

“It seems someone broke into the Iron Age Museum at Andover. All they stole was some silly piece of broken stone. The people in the museum don't even know what the thing was for." She shook her head in amazement at the pure stupidity of some individuals.

“Piece of stone?" repeated Chris, looking to Parrish for some sort of explanation. "Bit pointless, eh?"

"Probably." he agreed readily enough, although he didn't share the sentiment at all. "Still," he added. "I think I might go and take a look. Get me out of the house for a while and besides, it can't hurt."

“As you like." shrugged Lorraine non-commitally. "Now, can I have my paper back?"

The very next morning, on his first outing into the modern world since arriving at Chris's, Parrish visited the nearest Army surplus store.

Using his new found wealth he bought himself a new pair of boots and the latest windproof combat smock. SAS issue, the assistant told him, clearly expecting him to be impressed. Parrish just shrugged and inspected the garment closely before agreeing to buy it. Virtually the same as his old jacket apart from the higher tech material and its detachable hood, he felt immediately at home in it and quickly transferred all the contents of his old coat to the new one, including both flint daggers, the remaining pieces of jerky, assorted bits of dry tinder and other odds and ends. While in the shop he also added some small bits of kit to this collection, unable to resist passing up the chance to buy a Victorinox pocketknife and a new flint and steel. He handed the old jacket rather reluctantly to the shop assistant, who took it politely enough, waiting till the strange customer had left the shop before taking it straight out to the back yard and tossing it unceremoniously into the dustbin.

Now in clean new boots, fresh denim jeans, a black polo neck and smart new camouflage jacket, Parrish felt he didn't quite stand out so much now from the crowd.

Much easier to move unobtrusively about, he thought. Now, on to the next objective.

Finding the nearest taxi rank he approached the only vehicle there and looked down into the upturned face of its driver.

“Can you take me to Andover?" he asked.

"No problem, Guv." came the instantly cheery reply, the man's eyes lighting up at the prospect of a good fare, unusual during the middle of the day. Parrish climbed in.

No sooner had the car moved off than the driver launched into his friendly patter, announcing himself as Bob and beginning to shoot questions at his passenger. Parrish waited until the man had to pause for breath then cut in sternly.

“Just take me to the Iron Age Museum at Andover. And if it's all right with you, I'd like to travel there in peace and quiet."

“Huh!" grunted Bob. "No need to be rude. Only had to say. Just trying to be cheerful." He shrugged then grumbled on under his breath for a while longer before finally lapsing into silence.

Parrish paid him no more attention. He watched the countryside passing by outside as the vehicle sped on towards its destination, trying to spot any landmarks he might remember from the past. Although some of the rolling landscape seemed vaguely familiar, it seemed almost cluttered with the accoutrements of modern man, dotted as it was with houses and farm buildings and crisscrossed with telephone wires and the great, tall stanchions of the National Grid that seemed to stride in arrow straight lines across the landscape, all the time holding aloft thick wires humming with power. He thought it all looked a bit ugly now but once or twice still felt the need to open the window and hang his head out just to get a faint sniff of the outdoors. It was still distinguishable even though masked by the various scents of civilization, engine fumes and the sickly odour of the so called ‘air freshener' in the vehicle he was travelling in. The one that still never managed to mask the acrid tang of the drivers last cigarette.

Forty minutes later the taxi drew to a halt right outside the entrance to the museum. Parrish not only paid the fair but also gave a generous tip. As a thank you for observing his request for silence, he said. This gesture immediately cheered the driver, who rummaged briefly in the glove compartment before handing him a card.

"If you need any more quiet trips, Guv," he grinned. "Just gimme a shout."

"Thanks Bob. Will do." He gave the man a loose salute, watched the vehicle pull away then went into the building.

A small fee gained him entry and he spent the next twenty minutes wandering almost aimlessly around main galleries, trying to figure out just what had in fact been stolen.

Nearly all he could see that concerned his former home tended to concentrate on the Iron Age aspects of the hillfort. There were though some pictures that did give a rough guide to the original shape, size and strength of the encampment in earlier times. They weren't even all that close, Parrish knew. He did find one small display case showing a few unearthed arrowheads and the odd stone whorl. These made him pause for a moment as he remembered the people that had used them and it was then he began to think it might not have been such a good idea to come here after all.

Making his way back to the reception area he found himself alone apart from the lady behind the counter of the souvenir shop-cum-ticket booth. He hadn't noticed when he'd first entered but now, standing almost awkwardly in the middle of the foyer at a loss as to what to do next, he saw the lapel badge she wore. It proclaimed her as one of the museum curates. Relegated to shop assistant too by staff cuts, he didn't wonder.

"I was just curious," he broached, trying hard not to sound quite as interested as he really was. "It said in the paper that you'd been broken into not long ago?"

"Oh yes." said the lady, her eyes instantly lighting up. "Two days ago. The front door had been forced, there was glass everywhere and, what with the Police, oh, it was most exciting!"

"I was wondering just what exactly had been stolen? It must have been ever so valuable." Realizing that the woman truly was excited by the event, it was difficult for Parrish not to over act and sound as gullible as she.

The gullible one shook her head dramatically.

“Oh no, no. It was just an odd shaped piece of stone, broken down one side. Clearly just a fragment from a much larger piece."

“Shame I couldn't have seen it.” He sounded crestfallen, eyes lowered.

“That's all right." came the quick reply as she reached eagerly under the counter. "All out exhibits are photographed and catalogued. I've a picture of it here." She produced a fat book, already open at the correct page. He doubted he was the first to be shown the image.

“There." she said triumphantly, laying the book wide on the countertop and pointing with a thin finger. Both peered down at the crisp black and white image as if seeing it for the first time. The accompanying foot note was easily readable.

Hand worked stone, decorated with painted line, found inside the original defenses. Possibly from the late Neolithic period.

“No one really knows what it is." she announced.

I do, thought Parrish.

About the size of a building block, the piece of stone was smooth and slightly rounded on one side, a faint trace of dark paint clearly visible, while the other side was a jagged break where it had separated from the rest of the object.

Like a significant piece of a jigsaw, if it came with the accompanying picture, it was easy to see where the piece went and Parrish could put *this* piece to the whole exactly for he had lived daily in the shadow of such a thing for three years.

It was a section from one side of a Dannu statue.

“Are there any other pieces like this in the museum?" he asked. She shook her head.

“Not here. But I know the curator at the Devizes museum and he says there's a similar piece in their archive section. It's not displayed 'cos it's not a particularly interesting piece. And all the best pieces end up in the British Museum."

“I see ...” Parrish was now deep in thought. "Before I go, could you show me where the theft happened?"

She glanced briefly from side to side as if checking the emptiness around them for spies.

“I don't see why not. It'll only take a minute and no one will know. Don't you think it's awfully exciting too?" she added almost under her breath.

"Oh yes, awfully."

The sarcasm was totally lost on the now very bright eyed woman as she led Parrish through a doorway directly opposite the main entrance to the museum proper. He knew he had not as yet visited this section of the building. A short passage led to another door above which there was a sign in bold lettering.

STONE AGE ARTIFACTS OF DANEBURY

it announced proudly.

Parrish's eyes fell immediately on a glass cabinet to one side that had its end panel blanked off with cardboard and secured with parcel tape. The curate crossed to it, he followed and together they stared down into the display, eyeing the contents. There was an obvious gap where he stolen object had once lain. Around it were several other stone tools and artifacts, each with an accompanying typed label that guessed at rather than stated exactly what they were. Some were accurate while the Chieftain of Danebury grinned briefly at the wild guesses of the rest. But the grin did not stay for none of them held any interest to him.

He had hoped to gain more information to give him some insight into just what exactly was going on and what was expected of him. The objects before him were all just flint odds and ends he could have simply picked up off the ground back in his village. It all left him none the wiser. After gazing, apparently awe inspired, at the small collection for as long as he thought was required, he straightened up and turned to leave.

"Thank you" he nodded at the proudly grinning woman. "Thank you very…"

The words tailed off into silence as his attention was immediately caught by a larger glass cabinet across the room, unseen behind him as he had entered. Inside it lay a human skeleton, curled into a loose foetal position. The remnants of a small clay pot and a few flint pieces lay close around it.

In that first instant he was simply captured by the morbid curiosity that the living have with the dead, but it was more than just that. Parrish felt suddenly drawn to them. He strode across, peering briefly but intently down at the complete set of bones before reading the information card in the corner of the cabinet.

This complete skeleton was excavated from a Neolithic long barrow sited only half a mile north of Danebury hillfort. To be given an individual burial mound and interned with perhaps his most treasured possessions, which includes the flint weapons you now see beside him, this adult male must have been highly respected among the people of the time. Perhaps he was a great warrior or a leader of men?

It is not known for certain how he died but marks at the top of the spine indicate that the head appeared to have been removed from the body either just before or quite soon after death.

One curiosity is known though. If you look closely at the face of the skull, bone damage can clearly be seen. At some time in his life this man's nose had been very badly broken!

Parrish froze, stunned.

The curate watched in confusion as she saw the man place his fingers gently against the glass. Then his broad shoulders slumped and his head dropped ever, so slowly, until the face with the blue markings pressed gently down against the cold top pane.

“Are you all right?" she asked, moving quickly to his side.

“My friend!” whispered Parrish softly, his arms gently encircling the glass box as if in embrace.

"Sorry?" she frowned, not sure she had heard him correctly. Parrish straightened abruptly, his back all at once ramrod straight.

“Nothing." he said gruffly without looking at her, the harshness in his voice not quite managing to hide the quiver there. “Thank you. Goodbye." And with that he marched swiftly out of the room.

She heard the main door to the museum squeak shut on its dry spring as he left the building, but wasn't really paying attention. She was still trying to understand why there were suddenly what looked like fresh teardrops glistening on the top of the skeleton’s cabinet.

11

It was a deeply subdued Parrish who travelled in stony silence back to Southampton, the normally nose wrinkling odours inside the Andover Cabs car going unnoticed. In fact, Parrish wasn't even sure just how he'd arrived at the taxi rank in the first place, let alone hired a driver to take him back.

After dashing from the museum he had simply wandered aimlessly about, lurching emotionally from the shock and horror. True, he had sometimes wondered if one day, long after his death, he might be dug up by some unknowing archaeologist and put on display, but to actually *see* his friend like that ... The harsh reality of it all stabbed at his heart like a dagger. It was almost too much to bear and close behind the shock came an overwhelming feeling of the complete helplessness of his own situation. Everything combined to slide Parrish slowly into a state of soul crushing dejection.

Was it blind luck that led him to a nearby taxi rank or some mysterious, guiding hand that steered him there? Either way he was on his way back and the null time afforded him as he travelled allowed a breathing space for a recovery of sorts. By the time he was dropped off at his requested destination in the city suburbs he was once again on an even keel, the only obvious outward sign of his suffering was his battered optimistic outlook, now replaced with a scowling dislike of the time where he now lived and the harsh, uncaring and disrespectful society that lived here. It wasn't that he blamed any individuals for what had happened to people and their attitudes to death, other people or the planet itself. It was simply so obvious to him, and yet unseen by almost everyone else, that the human race was in fast decline towards decadence, anarchy and final self-destruction. It made him despise them for their complacency and himself for being a part of it.

Fighting against all this, his subconscious mind had tried to seek out for him a place of refuge from the emotional assault, a place of warmth where he might gain shelter from the pressing humanity and perhaps feel wanted again just for himself. And so it was quite a different type of shock to receive when he climbed from the cab to find himself, apparently at his own request according to the driver, on the corner of the street where he had grown up in what now seemed much more than a lifetime ago. Only a few doors down from where he now stood, opposite the small park where he'd kicked a ball around as a boy, was the house of his parents.

He realized it was another mistake, after visiting a place that concerned itself with one area of his past life, to then visit another place in the same field. He mentally admonished himself for allowing such blatant sentimentality to further cloud his judgment.

Even so, a small smile flitted briefly across the face of the Chieftain of Danebury as he walked those familiar pavement slabs before swinging away from the house at the last moment to cross the road and enter the park through a well-trodden gap in the low hedgerow that surrounded it.

He settled on a vandalized but still usable bench within the park that gave him an unobstructed view across the litter strewn grass, unkempt shrubbery and over the intervening road to the house of his youth.

It was a lot easier to settle his breathing than his troubled thoughts as he gradually became completely motionless, seeming somehow to merge with the park itself, there and yet unnoticed by others who every day saw, without seeing, the haven of green in the red brick jungle.

Parrish watched as only Dannu's man could watch.

Birds came and went, mostly feral pigeons and the all invading sparrows that scavenged for food. Vehicles passed in an intermittent yet never ending stream up and down the road between him and the center of his attention.

People passed by. Mostly mothers steering push chairs

loaded with either babes or shopping or both, and young children, little live wires of boundless energy fizzing around the park land like landlocked whirlygig beetles.

Occasionally a young teenage group swept by, moving in an untidy, noise drenched cluster. Old people also passed, at a much reduced speed, and Parrish thought how sad it was that very few held their heads proud and erect and how little, if any, respect they were offered by those around them. Here was humanity condensed. A window on this modern world passing before Parrish's all seeing eye. And as he watched all those around him, intent only on their own lives, little businesses and individual concerns, he was being passed over without so much as a second glance in his direction. He might as well have not been there at all. Just another tramp or down and out, someone who did not warrant any attention or concern. It was a tribute he realized, to the uncaring, dehumanization of his race in the lack of care for their fellow man.

Before this day, Parrish might have observed the goings on with a keen interest, interpreting all the information before him to gain some insight into the lives of these people. But now he gazed on impassively, with an aloof detachment that bordered on being ice cold. Like a scientist who might study microbes under a glass just to see what they did, uncaring as to how they did it or what the outcome of their actions might be.

Then all at once all this was pushed from his mind. He stiffened as a car slowed and pulled to a stop directly outside the house. He tried to smother the sudden excitement that welled within him as he instantly recognized the driving style. He knew his father sat behind the wheel.

The man climbed out and a woman emerged from the other side.

A full blown smile was on Parrish's face as he saw his parents, content for that moment just to gaze upon them though they were totally unaware of his presence, a moment to be savoured considering he had always accepted that it would never happen.

The elderly couple met at the front gate where the man held it open for his wife. Just like him, thought Parrish warmly, still watching motionless from his bench. They reached the front door and, after a brief fumble of keys, entered and were gone from sight.

The closing door coincided with the smile falling from Parrish's face, the dour look returning as his coldly assessing mind put together the pieces and understood the results.

They were much older, he thought. Older than he'd expected. Dad looked a lot more lined about the face and both he and Mum were considerably grey now. They still moved confidently enough but even from a distance Parrish had seen that they appeared somehow beaten. As if worn out by life and bowing down, being slowly crushed by the never ending pressure of everyday life.

At that moment he so desperately wanted to go to them. To run over there as fast as he could and tell them everything was all right. To hold his mother tight and feel the warm, strong grip of his father's handshake. But a big part of the crushing of their lives was down to him, he knew. Chris had told him they took the news of his death very hard, and the inquest hadn't helped either. It must have been terrible for them at the funeral too. Parrish understood now just how much damage he had inflicted on his parents, through no fault of his own. The bitterness he suddenly felt went deep into him. He wished now he'd not seen them at all, this damned world even taking from him his memories of past happy days with his parents. Days of optimism, excitement and hope at what the future might bring.

He rose slowly to his feet, took one last, wistful look at the house of his childhood, once full of fond memories, then turned his back and walked grim faced away across the park. Not once did he look back.

It was at that moment he really began to hate the twentieth century.

That evening Chris went up to Parrish's room to tell him his meal was ready. Unusually, Parrish had been nowhere to be seen when he and his wife had returned home from work. Lorraine didn't like shouting in the house so Chris obligingly trudged up the stairs, knocked and entered. He found Parrish sitting cross legged in the middle of the floor.

"Dinner's ready, mate." he'd said before sensing the atmosphere in the room. There was something in the air and he knew without having to ask that his friend had been brooding here all afternoon. His few words, cracking into the heavy silence like a brick through a window, suddenly seemed so trivial as he grasped the fact that something profound had befallen the seated man.

“Parrish?" Chris placed a hand on his friend's shoulder and the action seemed to drag the man from some sort of trance. He looked up into the others eyes. Chris studied the troubled face, looking for the reason but seeing only the result. Gone was the hint of that charming smile that usually lurked at the corner of the mouth, to be replaced by a hard, coldly calculating look in the eye.

“Are you OK?" There was genuine concern in Chris's voice. “What happened today? Did you find out anything?"

“Plenty." Parrish replied to the last question only, Chris catching the irony there but not understanding. He forced a smile and rose to his feet. “C'mon, let's go and eat and I'll tell you all about it.” he lied. That was something else he was finding easier to do now.

Over dinner he talked to his hosts about what he had discovered at the Andover Museum, omitting any reference to either his friends or family, living or otherwise. Chris seemed genuinely interested in the odd shaped piece of stone and quizzed Parrish about his next move.

Lorraine sat and ate in silence for the most part, merely listening politely to Parrish's words but totally unable to take her eyes off the man. She too could see the change in him only to her it held a completely different fascination. He looked more determined now. Hardened. The air he carried and the look in his eye bordered on brutal. She would of course never ask but didn't doubt that the man opposite her would be quite capable of killing if the mood took him. Had he ever killed before? The thought both chilled and thrilled her and as the two men spoke together she found herself comparing them. With a sudden, harsh honesty that shocked her she admitted she'd married Chris because he was a fit and good looking, work hard play hard action man. But now, seated opposite, was a *very* fit, genuine hard man with a scarcely disguised vicious streak she'd never seen before. There was now no denying the attraction she felt towards her husband's friend and, as it deepened and increased, she realized that in contrast her affection for her husband was diminishing.

At that very moment Parrish, whilst still listening to Chris, looked straight at her in an apparently casual gesture. She suddenly felt as if his piercing gaze could see straight inside her head and read her very thoughts. It made her flush red and she stared down at her food. After a few moments of attempting to gather herself, she looked back up. His gaze was still upon her and it was there in his eyes. Just how, she couldn't grasp but there was no denying the truth of it. He knew.

“What's your next move, Shaun?" Chris was asking.

In a seamless transition from one to the other Parrish returned his gaze to his friend.

"It's gotta be the Devizes Museum." he said evenly, to the amazement of Lorraine who could only marvel at his self-control. "Whoever stole the stone at Andover probably wants more pieces of the same type, for whatever reason."

He had a sudden thought and turned back to Lorraine. "Wasn't there something in that paper yesterday about the British Museum?"

"Yes!" she cried, jumping almost too eagerly out of her seat to retrieve the broadsheet, grateful to get out from under the man's invasive gaze. As she rummaged through the bulging magazine rack Chris continued.

“So you'll be going there tomorrow then? Need a lift? I can take a day off if you want help."

"No Chris, but thanks for the offer. You're already doing more than enough and I'm very grateful. Besides, I think an evening visit rather than during the day is in order this time. After two thefts," he raised an eyebrow to Lorraine, now rapidly scanning the pages of the paper in her hands, “I think whoever is responsible will have to be a bit more careful."

" Yes" she confirmed, speed reading the article. "Nothing specific here but it does say an obscure relic was taken." She was amazed to find herself actually pleased to be of some help to him.

“Tonight?" Chris too was suddenly keen. "I can run you over after dinner." The thought of real action again, after all these years, rekindled a thrill in him he'd not felt in a long time. And enjoyed. But he was to be disappointed, as Parrish answered.

"No, I'll sort out my own transport. I don't want you directly involved." He raised a hand, quelling any protests. "There could be trouble and with theft there usually comes the Police." He wanted to add dishonour too but they would never have understood. "Besides, tonight is not the right time. It's tomorrow night."

"But ... how could you know that?" Chris voicing both the others thoughts but letting any further protests go unsaid as they looked into his suddenly determined eyes. In all honesty Parrish wasn't exactly sure how he knew but something inside him insisted that he was right.

“I Dannu .. er .. dunno." he corrected himself. "Let's just say a little bird told me. Either way, I can do nothing until then I'm sure."

And with that, leaving both Chris and Lorraine confused and with many unanswered questions, he returned his attention to the food before him. The couple sharing his table, but not his thoughts, unexplainably felt as if they'd been dismissed.

12

The following evening, just as dusk was drawing in, found Parrish waiting to be picked up. He stood well back from the curb of the main northward drag out of Southampton that was The Avenue and was motionless except for the eyes that surveyed the passing traffic in an uncaring, detached way. His back was against a high, wooden paneled fence and under one arm he carried a dark coloured car blanket purchased earlier in the day.

It may have been easier to be collected from right outside Chris's house but Parrish still wished as few people as possible to know of his exact whereabouts, and so he'd walked free of the little crescent, used a public call box then made his way to the agreed rendezvous point.

A few moments later a taxi passed him before breaking hard to a halt. Fortunately the traffic was light during the mid-evening and the sudden action caused no trouble. Parrish recognized the vehicle, walked across to it and climbed into the rear passenger compartment.

“Hah! Nearly didn't see you then. Still, bang on time, eh?" said the driver cheerily, hoping for an encouraging acknowledgment from his latest fare. He got none, Parrish having no interest in minutes and hours. To him time was just continual and endless and the startling fact that he could travel up and down in it no longer impressed either.

"To Devizes, Bob." was his curt reply.

Sour as ever thought Bob but grinned cheerily again anyway. "Right oh, Guv."

"And my name is not 'Guv'." growled Parrish before he could stop himself. Realizing there was a hint of real venom in his voice was a shock. It seemed he was beginning to lose his self-control along with his 'live and let live' philosophy and had gotten angry at a trifling matter simply because he disliked it. And Bob had done no wrong, not deserving the harsh words. He was just being himself.

"Er ... right." Came the tentative reply. There was no mistaking his passengers barely concealed anger at him. Bob suddenly wondered if picking up this man might be a dangerous mistake. "Well, ... um ... did you say Devizes, Chief?" There was a moment's stony silence and Bob visibly trembled as he realized he'd innocently tacked another name generalization on the end of the sentence without thinking. The fear of violence began to show on his face but to his complete surprise Parrish finally smiled.

"Chief is close enough." There was genuine humour then. "And yes, I said Devizes. You know, in Wiltshire. Is that a problem?"

There was a pause as Bob considered. He had no doubt the man sharing his cab was a hard case right enough, probably capable of doing very nasty things, but he'd been taxiing now for a lot of years and reckoned himself a good judge of character. His gut instinct told him the big guy with the hard stare was OK and there was another momentary pause was while he silently searched for the right word to describe him. That old fashioned word, not used much nowadays. Honourable. Yes, that was it.

"No. No, I'll just have to radio in and let them know I'm on a long fare and'll be out of the city for a while is all." Bob settled back into his seat, eyeing Parrish momentarily in his rear view mirror before transferring his attention to the traffic outside. "Just settle back and make yourself comfortable, Chief."

This second innocent, unknowing acknowledgment of his position drew another small smile from the Chieftain of Danebury and with that Bob nodded, selected first gear and pulled away from the curb.

The night had fallen dark and starless, a detail Parrish noted to his satisfaction as he climbed from the taxi now halted in Devizes market square. Square was rather inaccurate as the tarmaced area was a road bordered, elongated triangle with shops lining the long north edge, the Victorian built council offices along it's short base and a pub-cum-hotel filling most of the south side. The Black Bear, normally a bland, flat faced building of grey stone, looked somewhat bleak in the orange glow of the street lights, the impenetrable night beyond a contrasting backdrop that soaked up any residual light like blotting paper. All this Parrish took in with a long, sweeping glance as he turned full circle before leaning in towards the driver's window, opened now to receive the fare.

“Bob," he said quietly. "Can you be back here to pick me up at the far end of the square at sunrise? Ah .. four thirty." he added, quickly adjusting his time scale to modern thinking, helped along by a quick glance at the dully illuminated clock face high up on the front of the council building.

"Well ..." Bob knew he would normally be working a shift in his home town at that time but was somehow loathe to say no to his quietly powerful, charismatic passenger. It just seemed to be something you didn't say tohim.

Parrish smiled.

“Both way fare of course, and fifty quid in your pocket if you're on time." Now there was no hesitation.

“I won't let you down, Chief.”

"Good man."

Parrish nodded, the deal done, paid Bob the fare price without another word then turned and walked slowly away across the square towards the pub. Tucked once again under his arm was the woolen blanket and Bob puzzled briefly on the item before pulling away, swinging across the square to rejoin the main road, passing between Parrish and the Black Bear at the start of his journey back across Salisbury Plain toward Southampton. He waved cheerily to the tall man as he swept by but the gesture was not returned.

Parrish waited till the vehicle was gone from sight, using the time to feel the air around him, before turning east and following the road out of the square, heading along it towards the Devizes Museum which he knew was somewhere ahead of him. Knew only because of the tourist information signpost on the corner of the square that told him so.

He found it easily enough, the 'MUSEUM ENTRANCE' sign

suspended above the door a dead giveaway. It was in the middle of a long line of Edwardian buildings on the right side of the street, their fascia's hard up against the pavement, harshly illuminated by the street lighting.

Just before he reached the Museum proper Parrish drew alongside an alley, actually a narrow driveway, that split the red brickwork. It was unlit but at the far end he could see it opened out onto an illuminated courtyard that fronted a residential block. He paid particular attention however to the small sign fixed on the left face of the alley wall just inside the entrance and still visible in the slanting street light.

MUSEUM STAFF ONLY - CAR PARK

Parrish nodded briefly in satisfaction then, after a quick look around to ensure no one was watching, stepped sideways into the driveway, effortlessly sliding from the medium of light into the domain of the dark.

There was no sound now as he moved. Perhaps halfway down the alley he came to the car park entrance, no more than a simple gap in the high brick wall allowing passage into the back yard.

The back of the building was as typically Edwardian as the front with several different levels of sloping roofs from ground floor scullery, through projecting stairwells right up to the steeply pitched roof. All the windows were timber framed sliding sash affairs in cracking and faded white gloss. Under his feet the car park was just a bare open space between the back of the building and the overgrown boarder and trees that lined the rear boundary. Rough and ready but good enough.

Parrish moved quietly to the shadow shrouded greenery and briefly explored. There was another high wall behind it but the cover was deep enough and he searched about until he located a suitable spot. One that allowed him an unobstructed view of the Museum but ensured he was out of sight. There he shook free the dark green woolen car blanket and, holding it by two corners, draped it around his shoulders. It wasn't the same as his cape, wasn't half as good as his cape, but it had a vaguely home feel about it and it surprised him just how much comfort he drew from the sensation. Making sure there was plenty of blanket beneath him for insulation against the cold ground he sat carefully down deep in the undergrowth in his chosen position. After a final check satisfied him that he could see but was himself unseen, he settled down to wait.

There were still a few hours to go before the dawn. A scavenging hedgehog had earlier sniffed curiously around the silent, unmoving living statue that blocked his usual route, before moving on around the obstruction. Apart from that there had been no activity at all.

Until.

Detecting movement, Parrish's eyes flicked left. It reminded him of waiting patiently near rabbit holes, weapon poised in readiness for the intended prey to appear. No matter how long and diligently he stared at a burrow, the animal always seemed to just suddenly be outside. Not once had he ever actually *seen* a rabbit emerge.

So it was now. As Parrish looked he saw a man inside the back yard not far from the gap in the wall. Never saw him enter, he just seemed to appear there. That meant that he was good. Real good.

The man was tall and had a good build, was Parrish's first impression, this easily noticeable even in the low light. Dressed from head to toe in black, he wore a black ski mask with slits for the eyes and mouth and a small dark knapsack hung limp across his back. He too made no sound as he moved across to the building, flattening up against the wall. Clearly having reconnoitered the place previously, he went gliding along the face of the wall ignoring one drainpipe to get to the next, then shinned up it and clambered deftly onto a sloping tiled roof that led up to one isolated window on the first floor.

Parrish had no way of knowing but this window allowed entry to the public area toilet of the Museum, directly beyond which was the Neolithic room of the pre-history displays.

The man in black moved up the smooth slope of the tiles managing to be both silent and to keep as much as possible in the shadow of the overhang of the roof above. It was impressive and Parrish couldn't help admiring the skill.

So silent was the whole scene that even from across the yard Parrish could hear the faint but crisp crackle of the glass cutter as it scored its way over the pane.

Moments later the window was slid up and the shadowy figure vanished into the inky blackness of the building's interior. Parrish waited briefly, knowing the man would take a precautionary glance back across the yard to check his escape was clear, before moving out of his hiding place to cut off that escape. He moved smoothly across the car park and slid into a shadow not too far from that second drainpipe and waited some more.

It didn't take long.

The sound of a smashing display cabinet an instant before the silence of the night was shattered by the blaring burglar alarm told Parrish the man had found what he was after. It also told him something about the burglar, who didn't feel the need for a stealthy exit and why the glass cutter hadn't been used a second time. It was only moments from the scene of the crime to a clean getaway and so, with the deafening noise, the satisfaction of violently of smashing towards the objective and even the faint chance of some unexpected police intervention, it all added to the thrill of the event. The man got off on the rush.

Parrish tensed as he heard the man in black slither down the tiles before dropping the last six feet to the ground, landing cat like only a few feet away, his back turned.

The Danebury man closed, noting briefly that the knapsack now hung with some weight, priming himself to overpower the thief. But somehow, even above the noise of the alarm, the man sensed his approach and without warning spun, lashing out with the stiffened edge of one hand. Parrish was almost caught completely unawares and only at the last moment managed to raise an arm to protect his exposed throat. Partially deflecting the blow, he took the chop across the side of the face, his cheekbone carrying the brunt of it. The force of the strike made him stagger back against the wall and his opponent took full advantage, allowing no time for recovery. Parrish's legs were savagely kicked from under him and he crashed to the ground, just managing to turn his back as the anticipated boot came in for the killer blow. Not connecting with his head, it drove hard into his shoulder blade, driving the air from his lungs. His assailant gave out a hiss of annoyance before putting in a second kick, this one more expertly aimed, into his lower back. Pain exploded inside Parrish as the heavy boot crashed into his spine and kidneys. His agonized gasp seemed a more acceptable result to his attacker, who let out a brief laugh of satisfaction before sprinting away across the car park and out through the gap in the wall, his assault boots still making surprisingly little noise.

It took a few moments for Parrish to gather himself before he could find his feet and chase after the man, moving as quickly as he could with his head ringing and one hand pressing against the pain in his lower back. But too many vital seconds had been lost and even before he reached the mouth of the driveway he heard an engine firing up. Fearing his one lead to be lost, he ran out into the street as an accelerating car approached. Its lights were at that moment still off but Parrish caught a glance of the front number plate as a sudden beam of light cut across the vehicle, lancing down from a bedroom window, the room's occupant aroused by the din from the alarm. To his surprise, at the same moment the cars head lamps were thrown onto dazzling high beam, he heard the downshift and the saw vehicle swerved towards him, engine gunning. With a gasp of horror he threw himself back into the mouth of the alley, feeling the slipstream of air as it roared by.

There was a slight scrape as the driver slightly misjudged his approach and clipped the edge of the building before making good his escape as he roared off into the night, leaving Parrish sprawled and panting on the ground in the dark alley, just the constant clamour of the alarm for company.

13

Bob pulled into the market square just after first light.

The taxi man had been driving professionally now for over fifteen years and had seen on his travels many strange, sometimes downright weird and occasionally some amazing things. The evident police activity at the side of the road by the Devizes Museum therefore only warranted a cursory glance as he passed by.

Bob was getting better at spotting the hard man who was waiting once again in patient silence, not much more than a solid shadow in a convenient doorway. He pulled up alongside and Parrish moved smoothly and swiftly across the pavement and climbed inside. For some reason the absence of the blanket registered smartly on Bob's mind. The way it had been carried the previous night was as if it had held some secret value. Yet now it was as if his passenger had never owned such an item. He thought it best not to mention it.

“Back to Southampton, Chief?" He asked in the best cheery voice he could manage at this early hour.

"Yes."

“Er ... Southampton where, exactly?"

"Where you first picked me up from will do." came the curt reply.

Not once had Bob turned in his seat to look directly at Parrish and now he slightly adjusted his rear view mirror to catch the man's eye, once again wary of any impending trouble. All he saw there in the glass was a troubled look. That and a slight discolouration around the cheekbone and up towards the eye as a bruise was beginning to appear.

Parrish was aware of the attempt at eye contact and offered the briefest of smiles in return then nodded.

Bob nodded back, somehow reassured, before re-adjusting his mirror and moving off, a few moments later passing once again the Museum and the police activity surrounding it, flashing blue lights and all.

"Looks like bother." Bob said, rather non-concerned with the incident itself, just attempting to make conversation. "Most likely a break in. Huh! Who'd want to burgle a Museum?"

“I wouldn't know." said Parrish flatly before dropping into a heavy silence, and it nagged Bob all the way back that he thought somehow the Chiefs answer wasn't all that convincing.

Chris had risen early, or at least what he considered to be early, and made his way to the bathroom assured of having it to himself, only to be confronted by the sight of Parrish, stripped to the waist, bending over the sink.

“Been up long?" he asked, somehow not too disappointed that the room was occupied because it was by his old friend.

Parrish straightened, stifling a grunt as pain stabbed at his lower back, and turned to face Chris.

“A while." he replied with a gentle grin, slowly removing the cold flannel he had been holding to the side of his face. The bruise on his cheek was beginning to glow and he'd be lucky if it didn't reach his eye and develop into a real shiner.

“Ouch!" Chris winced, then laughed. “What did the other bloke look like?"

Parrish laughed with him, for a brief moment enjoying the old camaraderie between them. Happiness was something he was finding harder and harder to come by nowadays.

“I wish." he grinned, with more than an element of truth. "Actually, it was my own fault, I've been up quite a while and didn't want to put on any lights in case it woke you. The place is still strange to me and I just stumbled into a door frame.”

Chris shook his head sadly. Parrish wasn't sure whether it was in disbelief or sympathy.

"Lorraine'll soon be up. She's a whizz with the first aid. Let her have a look at it. Now, if you've finished, clear off and let me get to the bathroom. I've gotta be at work in little over an hour."

“Sure, but .. er .. one thing Chris?"

"Mum?"

“Could you do something for me? I need to check out a car registration. Maybe you could put me on to someone or at least point me in the right direction. It's not something I ..."

“I think I can do better than that." Chris interrupted. "I actually know someone in the police force who might do me a favour if I asked. In fact, you'd know ..."

"Don't tell me!" Parrish cut his friend off. "I don't want to know and you're not to tell anyone else why the information is wanted or who wants it, is that understood?"

"But Shaun, it's ..."

“No one." growled Parrish, a hint of menace there this time. "Remember your promise. You gave me your word."

Chris shrugged then nodded and Parrish allowed another smile, patting him on the shoulder.

"Good man."

It wasn't a patronizing gesture and the men eyed each other for a long moment then smiled together. Friends. Parrish produced a scrap of paper from his pocket and handed it to Chris, who briefly scanned the registration number then tucked it away into a pocket of his own.

“Consider it done." he said then slid past Parrish to get at the sink. "And get Lorraine to take a look at that face."

“Did someone speak my name?" Lorraine at that moment emerged from the master bedroom, wrapped in a silk kimono style dressing gown the hem of which practically dragged on the carpet. Parrish met her as he stepped out of the bathroom and into the hallway.

"Yeah." Chris spoke without turning, gazing into the mirror intent on working a lather onto his face. As he spoke little spots of shaving foam spattered the glass. "Parrish has whacked his eye. Can you do anything for him?" He was totally oblivious to his wife who now stared transfixed while Parrish revealed once more his bruised face from behind the wet flannel.

The gesture initially went unnoticed. Lorraine wasn't looking at the man's face, her eyes hungrily drinking in the sight of his body as the Chieftain of Danebury stood expectantly before her, naked from the waist up. There wasn't an ounce of fat on him. His muscles were hard and knotty. Powerful. And they were somehow highlighted by both the crude tattoo work on his arm and neck and the dreadful white, ragged scars that slashed across the base of his neck, over his shoulder and along most of the length of his forearm. She was aware of a sudden dryness in her throat.

Parrish looked back at Lorraine, seeing the sudden awe in her eyes and also aware of her nipples coming sharply erect beneath the clinging silk. A moment later he could smell her too. Giving nothing away he just offered her a disarming smile and, pushing forward the injured cheek, said softly.

“What do you think?"

“I ... I think ..." Lorraine somehow gathered herself together. "Er ... I think we'd better put some witch hazel on that." She coughed nervously.

“Good idea." called Chris from inside the bathroom.

"If you think it'll help." said Parrish.

Lorraine reached out, hesitated for a moment then grasped Parrish by the arm, the first time she had actually touched him.

"Come on." she said evenly, more back to her brisk, self-assuredness now. "The medical box is down in the kitchen."

And with that she led off down the hallway, momentarily reluctant to release her grip on Parrish as they negotiated the stairs. She attempted one more time to show that she was not affected by his presence.

"Those scars." she asked, almost too casually. "What happened?"

“Wolves." he replied, matter-of-factly.

“Ask a stupid question." she muttered.

It was that very evening when Chris produced the information on the car number he'd been given. It seemed that somehow things were beginning to gather momentum.

After having slept, Parrish spent the rest of the day listening to the news bulletins on the radio, noting with satisfaction that the break in at Devizes had not once been mentioned. He expressed genuine surprise at the quick result of his friends work and Chris typically waved away the praise, simply reminding Parrish of how fast everything happens now with computers.

"When you get nicked for speeding nowadays the Old Bill have checked your plate before you've even stopped rolling."

he said, speaking from first-hand experience.

“Any problems with it?"

"Not really." Chris casually waved his hand again as if getting restricted information was something he did every day. "But our ... my friend was very curious as to why I wanted to know about this number in particular. Don't worry though, I didn't tell and he knows how to keep shtoom."

“So what did he say?" Even Lorraine was curious now. This was something she didn't experience every day.

“Well ...” Chris paused to enjoy the moment of having their undivided attention. "The car, a very flash BMW I might add, belongs to one mister Steven Tench." He pulled a single, jaggedly torn piece of lined note paper from his pocket and briefly checked his facts. "Seems he's a bit of a rough lad from all accounts. Several charges for GBH and ABH but no convictions. Ex-military as well but that's all my friend would say. I got the distinct impression I was only given the bare bones and that's not all He was dead curious to know why *I* should be interested in this mister Tench. It seems to me the police have got their eye on him as well as you, Parrish."

Something flashed across Chris's face as he glanced at Parrish's bruise, although the witch hazel was doing good work and the discolouration was already beginning to fade. Lorraine had even remarked on just how quickly he seemed to heal. He was a very fit and healthy man.

“Anyway," Chris continued. “There was no home address, at least none that they were prepared to divulge, although it appears he does frequent a certain night club in the city. The Shadow. A high class place mate, do you know it?"

“I can find it." said Parrish calmly.

“It's near St. Michael’s square." volunteered Lorraine.

“That's all the info I could get, mate." Chris shrugged and handed his friend the scrap of paper. “Is that OK?"

Parrish nodded, glancing down at the neatly written notes. It was enough. Tomorrow night he would try again to have a quiet word with this elusive mister Tench.

14

The Shadow, in complete contrast to its name, was bathed in bright light.

More a casino than a nightclub, it's bold facade of clean white stone, huge arching windows and the wide flight of steps leading up from a narrow courtyard to the central double doored entrance was starkly illuminated by skillfully placed arc lights.

To the right of the casino stood a building older and grander, the curved sweep of Cunard house, once an opulent hotel catering to those rich enough to enjoy its grandeur before embarking on those luxurious cruises of a long gone age.

Left of the casino was a row of town houses, separated from the white building by a poorly lit alley along which cars occasionally travelled en route to the casino's rear car park.

All this Parrish observed as he stood in a darkened doorway opposite.

His vantage point was the entrance of a pub now closed, it being long after midnight, the recessed doorway black against the brightness before him as the Chieftain continued his watch. His attention centered on the two bouncers who flanked the entrance, supposedly vetting those patrons wishing to enter. In fact, they hardly turned anyone away bar the blatantly obvious drunkards. After the pubs and clubs had chucked out those so drunk as could hardly stand either staggered home or slept where they fell while the genuine nighthawks arrived smart, bright and keen in the hope of success at the gaming tables. The bouncers were not much more than burly and, for the most part, polite doormen.

Parrish waited for a lull in the slow stream of visitors to the club and, with the street all at once empty, stepped out of the shadows and crossed the street. He did not consider himself improperly dressed to enter such a place. It did not cross his mind at all for what he wore was more or less all he had. His new combat boots were clean, as were his black jeans and the polo neck bought for him by Lorraine, snug around his throat. But his combat jacket immediately caught the attention of the bouncers as he approached, causing them both briefly to wonder where in the blazes he had suddenly appeared from.

Not pausing at the foot of the steps Parrish ascended, sizing up the two men as he drew near. Both wore dinner jackets and crisp white shirts which served to emphasize their bulging chests and huge physiques. The man on the left was older, perhaps late thirties and slightly balding. He moved easily but deftly to cover 'his' door. There were no sudden movements and his eyes studied Parrish for any signs of aggression, malice of evidence of weapons. He was a professional and good at what he did. Parrish actually liked him for that.

The man to the right was young. No more than twenty two or three. With a neatly trimmed Para-style moustache and a truly bulging physique that marked him as a keen bodybuilder, he was almost bursting out of his jacket. No doubt it impressed the girls but Parrish hardly even considered him a threat. All size but no power. A poser. Likewise, this man moved to cover 'his' door but in contrast to his partner he was brash and bold, standing with legs wide and arms away from his sides.

He opened then clenched his fists several times. It didn't faze Parrish, there was no aggression there, it just served to further pump up his arm and shoulder muscles.

The pair formed a broad barrier across the club entrance, effectively closing the open doors with their bodies well before Parrish reached the top of the steps. Approaching slowly with hands in full view he glanced briefly at Moustache before addressing Balding.

“I'd like to go in." he said quietly, no inflection in his voice. Just stating the fact.

“I'm sorry sir." replied the older man, the apology in his voice sounding genuine enough. "But you're not properly dressed and I don't think you intend to play the tables. And that's all that goes on inside here."

It was plain enough and reasonable enough but Parrish pressed on. Perhaps an explanation of sorts would gain him passage. He spoke slowly. Patiently.

“I need to get in. I am looking for a Mister Tench and have been told he is here."

Baldings eyebrows shot up at the mention of Mister Tench but before he could reply young Moustache stepped forward, gripped Parrish by the arm at the back of his bicep and said roughly.

“Can't you take a hint, soldier boy? Clear off now before I throw you down these steps to help you on your way."

There was a moment’s stony silence.

The look in Parrish’s eyes changed and recognition of it sprung to Baldings face just as Parrish turned his gaze to the younger bouncer. The older man stepped smartly up beside his partner, pushed him deftly aside with one broad shoulder and carefully removed the young man’s hand from Parrish’s arm. Ignoring the look of total shock on the moustached face he stood squarely before Parrish. Their eyes met, and held.

“Look." he said quietly. "We don't want any trouble. I give you my word that Mister Tench is not inside. We've been on duty since before midnight and he's not come up these steps. Try the car park at the back. Sometimes he arrives early but doesn't come in for a long time. Does deals there I think." he added, not sure why he felt he must explain quite so fully to this stranger.

“Deals?" Parrish kept his eyes on Balding but all the time aware of the youngster who just continued to shoot baffled glances at his partner.

"Yeah. I don't know what exactly. Safer not to ask."

Parrish looked over the man's shoulder into the blackness of the casino entrance then at the faces of both men before returning his gaze to Balding.

"I believe you. Thanks." He nodded briefly to the man then, without so much as an acknowledgment to his young accomplice, turned away and headed off down the steps.

“Yeah!" The youngster called loudly after him, doing his best to recover his lost composure. "And don't come back or else!"

"Shut up!" snapped the older man before letting out a sigh of relief.

"What?"

"You're a prat." he added. "Learn to read a man before you challenge him or you gonna spend a lot of time on the sick." Moustache looked totally baffled so the older, wiser man explained. This was to be a lesson in life. "Did you look into his eyes?"

"Yeah?"

"And what did you see?"

"Nothin'."

"You're half right but you didn't look hard enough." The older man moved closer. "He wasn't afraid for a start, or didn't you notice that? But there was something else. And I've seen it before." He paused, momentarily looking off into the past.

"Where?" asked Moustache.

"In the Falklands."

"You were there?"

"Yeah, and the look I saw there, I've just seen again in that man's eyes."

"What look?" The young man's voice was now quiet with respect.

"The eyes of a real killer. Some of the paratroopers I met who'd been involved in hand to hand fighting with the enemy. They had it. And he has it." The older man nodded down towards Parrish, now at the bottom of the casino steps. Moustache also stared down at him.

"D'you mean men who like to kill? Get some sort of buzz out of it?" he whispered.

"No. I don't think they like to kill. But they know without question that they're damned good at it. That man down there is in a completely different league to you and me. If we get into a fight and loose, then we'd expect to take a beating and maybe a trip to the hospital. Fight with that man and loose, and he would take away your life."

They both watched in silence as the man in the combat jacket moved to the edge of the building and turned into the side alley. As he did so and passed into the first puddle of dark shadow he seemed to just blink out of sight, gone without a sound.

The two bouncers stared on into the impenetrable blackness for a few moments before returning to their posts either side of the doors. Silence reigned for a while then, without looking at his partner, the young bouncer said simply,

"Thanks."

Unaware of the conversation going on above him Parrish moved down the alley noting without interest the high blank wall to his right and the shambling six foot high wooden fence to his left. Broken and missing slats along its length created gaping holes through which he could see the end of a short garden belonging to the first house and behind that the derelict, overgrown and sprawling wasteland of a disused railway yard. The sole illumination came from the few unbroken lights mounted high up along the casino wall. They threw intermittent puddles of watery light into the otherwise blanketing darkness.

The casino went back further than Parrish had supposed from his earlier observations while out front, and the alternate dark, light, dark of the alley made it seem even longer still. Emerging at the far end he cast his eyes across the graveled car park finding it much better illuminated, no doubt for the benefit of the security camera perched high on its mounting on the farthest corner of the building directly away to Parrish's right. Like it, he too scanned the plot, but only in search of one particular car. It was just about possible to see all the vehicles from the alley mouth and, with no wish to be caught on camera unless absolutely necessary, he stayed close to the corner. He mentally scoffed at the idea of the high cost of installing surveillance equipment to guard people's cars but not bothering to fork out the few pennies needed for replacement bulbs to light the alley the people then had to walk up after parking their precious vehicles.

Disappointment was just beginning to settle on Parrish's shoulders as he realized the car he wanted was not in sight, when a sudden shaft of bright light cut across the car park, throw by the opening of a door at the rear of the casino. A kitchen porter emerged struggling with the loaded black bin bags hanging from his clenched fists.

Dumping the bags unceremoniously beside an already overflowing dustbin the man briefly eyed the security camera, threw it a loose salute the produced a packet of cigarettes and box of matches from one pocket.

Parrish could hear the faint whine as the camera swiveled

away to scan the car park, effectively turning its back on the man taking an illicit break. This obvious arrangement between the security and kitchen staff brought a brief smile to Parrish's face before he too took advantage of it and moved quietly up beside the smoker.

“'S'cuse me." He said loudly, seeming to appear as if by magic at the man's side.

“SHIT! What the f....” Jerking in fright, the sentence remained unfinished as the porter convulsed into a great fit of coughing caused by the unexpected deep inhalation of smoke. Parrish clapped the man on the back, steadying him with the other hand and feigned laughter at the man's predicament.

“Sorry mate." he said in what he hoped was a friendly tone. "Didn't mean to startle you." he lied. “I only wanted a quick word.”

Wiping his watering eyes with a grimy sleeve and trying to bring his coughing under control the man turned to find the stranger between himself and the warm safety of the kitchen door. He laughed nervously.

“You, ah, you just, just made me jump like." he gasped before coughing one last time to clear his lungs as best he could. "Just having a quick smoke is all."

“No problem." Parrish nodded as if in approval to the man's 'anything you can get away with' attitude and gave a knowing wink. "I just wondered if you could help me. I'm looking for a Mister Tench. I was told he'd be here tonight but I don't see his car anywhere."

"Mister Tench!" repeated the man in an awed voice, eyed Parrish for a second then, lowering his voice as if afraid to be overheard, offered some advice. "You don't want to mess with him, mate. Last bloke that messed with him spent two weeks in the dentist's chair. Mister Tench is pretty handy, if you know what I mean."

Parrish briefly touched his still tender cheek. "Really? Anyway, it's nothing like that. Business." He winked again.

“Oh, right." The porter nodded then winked too as if he knew what it was all about. "Well, you won't find him here tonight and besides, I think his motor must be in for repair. I see it was dented the other night. I tell yah, if someone else other than Mister Tench done the damage, God help 'em." He shook his head sadly.

"Will he be back soon? Maybe in the next few days?" Parrish had to ask even though he knew it a forlorn hope. What would a kitchen porter know about the habits of an obvious villain with an apparently fearful reputation.

“I ain't got the faintest idea but if you really need to find him he won't be far from that bloke wot won all the money. Word has it he's taken on Mister Tench as a sort of bodyguard. You know, to keep all the beggars, scroungers and con-artists at bay."

“What bloke with all the money?" Parrish tried not to sound too interested.

“Where you been, mate?" asked the porter incredulously. "Don't you read the papers or go outside much? You know, that local bloke, I dunno his name, wot went to all the bookies and bet on the weather doing strange things. Then low and behold, about two weeks ago it pisses down with rain. Then there's thunder and lightning and bloody great gales and stuff. And he didn't just get it right to the day but almost to the hour according to some of the papers.

Course all the bookies give him really long odds against something like that happening and when it all did he really cashed in. It was really amazing."

Parrish just stood in silence, frozen to the spot, a cold realization gripping him as he began to put some of the pieces together.

“You all right, mate?" The kitchen porter interrupted the strangers train of thought.

“Er, yes. Fine." Parrish fixed the man with a suddenly determined stare. "Where can I find this man?"

The porter shrugged.

"He lives somewhere out near Romsey in a big house I think. But like I said, to see him you'd have to go through Mister Tench and he's a bit handy, like."

" Yes, yes, but where?"

“Dunno myself." The man shrugged again then raised a forefinger as if struck by a rare, good idea. "But I bet you could find out from a recent paper. They all covered the story you know 'cos it was a big win. And I mean big. Like hundreds of thousands ..."

“Thanks." Parrish clapped him absently on the shoulder. "Thanks a lot. You've been a great help."

Without waiting for any reply, he spun on his heel and walked off back toward the entrance of the alley.

“You’re welcome." the porter called after him. "Just watch out for that Mister Tench though ..."

But Parrish was deep in thought and if he heard the piece of advice he never acknowledged it, just turning away from the light of the car park as the porter looked down at his un-smoked cigarette, took one quick drag, stamped it out and went back inside.

Parrish had not gone too far back down the alley, still pondering his next move, when he felt them.

Hunters in the night.

Before he had the chance to go back, two men emerged through gaps in the wooden fence, one ahead and one behind him, blocking any escape.

To the unwary they would still be little more than dark shadows among the dark shadows. But Parrish had known the darkest night. Looking a few degrees off to the side and using his peripheral vision he watched the two maneuvering quietly for the best positions. In defense he moved slowly back against the high wall, then sidled along it till he stood centered beneath one of the working lights and its circle of illumination. Now the men had a choice to make. Show themselves, or move off in search of easier prey.

To his surprise they never even paused, both moving readily and confidently forward until standing just inside the circle of light, not more than ten or twelve feet away. It was then, as he saw their faces, that he understood.

Recalling the bouncer’s words about him not looking like wanting to enter a casino with the appearance of having neither money nor possessions, he was clearly poor fodder for a robbery. Then, he knew. This was no mugging, this was for fun.

Not hunters.

Scavengers.

Parrish didn't bother to point out that he indeed had no money. He just waited for their next move, slowly reaching into his combat jacket pocket.

The thug to his left saw the arm movement and swung his

own right hand into view. It held a long Bowie type knife with a wickedly curved blade.

“Now don't do nuffing stupid." he hissed, face a half leer. "Or I'll have to cut you up real bad."

His partner guffawed at that, dropping a three foot length of chain into view, jangling it for added effect. They both closed.

When they were almost within striking distance the knife man noticed the lack of terror on Parrish’s face and raised one eyebrow.

“Hey, this one thinks he's tough." he called to his partner, at no time taking his eyes off Parrish. There was an almost happy expectancy in his tone. This one promised to be even more fun than usual. "Well, go on then, tough guy. If you've got somefing in there, pull it. Let's see what you've got."

Parrish withdrew his hand from his pocket and held it out under the light, for all to see. A short length of stick with a flat, leaf shaped piece of stone lashed to the end.

"That's it?" asked the knife man sarcastically, a smile coming to his face.

The man with the chain guffawed again and the knife man's grin widened.

"If that's all you got, boy are you in *big* trouble." He thought it was a good joke.

So did the man with the chain. He guffawed for a third time and the knife man nodded at this appreciation, tilted his head back and laughed out loud.

At that moment, as he momentarily lost eye contact, Parrish leapt at him, closing in a blur of speed. Defensively pushing aside the big knife with a sweep of his left arm and stepping in close, he slashed back handed across the exposed throat with the keen edged flint knife. His or Klud's? The thought flashed briefly in his mind as both the man's throat and left side carotid artery gaped wide. Blood jetted, splashing unheeded onto Parrish as the man gargled, dropped the knife and clutched futilely at his severed throat, a shocked look freezing onto his face as he slumped to his knees before crashing to the tarmac.

Parrish had no time to witness the man's death throws. A stunning blow across the shoulder blades sent him staggering, the breath almost driven from his lungs. Turning in readiness to defend himself against the next strike of the chain, he seized his next chance as the second man paused, looking down in horror at his partner, only then realizing just what had happened and stunned by the bloody sight. Parrish in contrast was no stranger to blood or death and moved without hesitation. He leapt on the man, grabbing the arm that held the chain with his left while driving his own knife straight in through his opponent's ribs with the other. They both fell to the ground without further struggle, Parrish knowing without having to check that his strike had gone straight to the heart.

The second man died without sound and Parrish held him in embrace for a moment to be sure, before rising clear of the body, attempting to pull out his dagger as he did so. But the weapon was somehow lodged between the ribs and with a firm twist he pulled a second time. The blood soaked shaft pulled out with a soft 'plop' and Parrish glanced unappreciatively down at the bare stick in his fist, the flint head left buried deep inside the dead man's chest cavity. Poor lashings, he noted. The knife must be his.

Standing over the two bodies Parrish felt no remorse. They'd had their chance to leave but came on with confident intent, a confidence no doubt gained through previous attacks on other, more defenseless unfortunates. A fatal error of judgment. The Chieftain of Danebury was quite capable of looking after himself.

Casting the useless knife shaft away over the fence, Parrish slipped quietly out of the puddle of light without so much as a backward glance, the only movement then the slow, glistening spread of blood pooling out from under the corpses. Moving on to the end of the alley Parrish took a brief second to check that the street was empty then slipped away, quickly lost to the darkness of the night.

15

Lorraine came awake, disturbed by unexpected sounds from within the house, and rolled slowly over to eye glowing red digits of the alarm clock.

5.05 am

The early morning light was doing its best to get around the edges of the patterned curtains that kept the bedroom in a twilight state.

She remembered Chris disturbing her slumbers when he'd risen over an hour before. Early shift, he'd said the evening before. A rush job of some sort that needed to be completed and made ready to be shipped before midday. And so he was up and gone at the crack of dawn and wouldn't be home again until about two in the afternoon. The quiet noises persisted though and pushed her, much against her will, into full consciousness. She heard taps being turned and water running. A bath. Then those unmistakable soft cloth sounds of someone either dressing or undressing. Although quiet, the sounds became almost immediately unbearable to one such as her and she hurled back the covers and sat up in bed, a bad mood falling almost too easily into place. Her ignorant husband had left the bedroom door ajar and the bathroom was right next door. The sudden, hot hiss of the shower was the final straw.

“Parrish!" she growled, as if the man's name was a curse in itself.

Climbing naked from the bed she threw her dressing gown around herself and, holding it closed with one hand, flung wide the bedroom door and stamped down the corridor to the bathroom. That door too was ajar. She slammed it back with the heel of her free hand and swept in, ready to give Parrish a savage verbal broadside.

The harsh words died before they had lived, her pursed lips instead opening in slack jawed bewilderment.

Parrish had not heard her enter, stood as he was beneath the driving spray of the shower head, his back toward the door.

Briefly noticing the long, hot looking welt that ran diagonally down across his shoulder blades where he had been struck by the chain wielding thug, Lorraine was just in time to see the last of the blood washing from him, racing in diluted rivulets down his back to pool at his feet before swirling away down the plug hole. The totally unexpected shock of this caused her to not fully recognize his nakedness. Her gaze also briefly took in the small pile of odds and sods on the floor between the shower and the bath. They marked where Parrish had set down the contents of his jacket pockets before placing the jacket itself into soak in the tub. With a magnetic pull she could not resist, her eyes became fixed on the sodden heap of camouflage pattern cloth that sulked there in the red water, slowly releasing more and more dried blood into the hot liquid that was, even as she watched, becoming ever darker.

Parrish felt her nearness rather than heard her gasps and turned, saw her gazing fixedly, almost mesmerized into the bath, and quickly turned off the shower. He stepped out, knotted a towel at his waist and moved to her side. Still she did not seem to notice him there. She could not pull her gaze from the contents of the bathtub and he had to physically turn her by the shoulders till she faced him.

“Are you all right?" There was genuine concern in his voice.

With a tremendous effort Lorraine squeezed her wide eyes shut then opened them slowly and looked up at him.

“Ah ... yes ...I think so. Are, are you? I mean, the blood..."

"I'm fine." He tried to sound as soothing as he could and offered a smile.

She smiled back then. A small smile but the right response. She was recovering quickly, he could see. Her hard headedness was for once a help.

“But all this blood everywhere. You're not hurt?"

“No." Parrish released his hold on her shoulders and moved towards the door as he spoke, carefully yet apparently casually drawing her away from the sight of the blood. "I'm definitely OK. It's not my blood."

“But who's then?" She followed without realizing and he led her out into the corridor and along to his own bedroom door.

Parrish answered without looking back.

"I had some trouble with a couple of muggers, but it's sorted now."

“But there's so much blood, just off of your clothing." cried Lorraine. "Do you mean to say you put then both in hospital?"

Parrish entered his room and walked to the foot of the unused bed before turning, leaning nonchalantly against it and saying quietly, "No. When it was all over they were beyond medical help."

"You mean ... you ..." the unfinished sentence ended in a gasp as the full meaning of his words struck home.

Parrish just nodded, his only thought at that moment that the miserable victims should be grateful. At least their skulls wouldn't end up as additional trophies in his stall. With that he remembered just exactly where and when he was and only then did his face harden.

Lorraine could do nothing but stand and stare at this strange man before her. This killer before her. And was shocked to find she was not afraid. The revelation of her feelings astounded her. She was not afraid, she was *thrilled!*

She looked at him and soaked up what stood before her in the light of her new awareness as she fully saw the man for the first time.

Wet and all but naked, she saw.

The ragged scars on his neck, arm and leg. The brutish tattoos around his throat, on his face and arm that she now realized suited him, were part of him. His undeniable fitness and firm assuredness spoke volumes but not as much as the quiet yet fierce pride in him. But most of all she finally saw his aura of raw power. A power of life or death.

It swamped her and the need she had been finding more and more difficult to quell within her rode roughshod over her other feelings of shock, horror and amazement and now rose unchecked to the surface. As Parrish watched in a bemused silence the changing emotions as they crossed her face, she slowly approached, eyes locked on his, until she stood right up against him.

Tentatively at first, as if he might be red hot to the touch, she placed her palms on his chest and inhaled deeply, as if trying to absorb some of his power and charisma.

Parrish just had time to read the explosion of fire in her eyes before, with one hand she sharply whipped his towel away, pushed him backwards onto the bed, threw herself on top of him and smothered his mouth with urgent kisses, all the time grasping and tugging at his naturally responding manhood. She wanted him, needed him with a desperation that would not, could not be denied.

Parrish didn't overtly respond yet neither did he reject her. But then he doubted she would have paid much heed either way. Her obvious need was so great that she would have taken a lot of stopping and it was only Parrish's refusal to struggle against her wishes preventing the act from being an actual rape.

After kissing him almost hard enough to bruise both their mouths and long enough to feel the man come to full hardness in her hands, Lorraine knelt up above him and threw off her loosely flapping dressing gown. She briefly displayed her body to him, wanton sexuality firing on all cylinders. Parrish's eyes travelled up her body and she twitched and quivered as if they were physically touching her, from the moistness of her groin, up past her shapely waist and over her smoothly rounded, jutting and heaving breasts. But this was not the time for pause. She was driven now by a deep animal desire, showing as much in the wild glint in her eyes as by the obvious language of her body.

Positioning herself above his hips she gripped his hardness aggressively at its base then plunged down onto him. She was so wet with desire there was almost no resistance at all and she gave a deep sigh of pleasure at her initial feeling of sexual success. Now she grasped either side of his chest along the base of his ribcage and, with a thrusting motion that started high up in her shoulders, began urgently stroking up and down on him gasping and throwing her head back as the unstoppable desire gripped hard. So urgent was her need that she reached orgasm in a matter of moments. Parrish could do no more than look on in astonishment as Lorraine seemed to peak almost immediately upon engulfing him, a great shriek springing from her throat as her body erupted.

The cry died away to gasps before she recovered her breath enough to lift her hanging head and eye Parrish with a shining new desire to take them both to the peak this time. With that target in mind, she settled back onto his manhood more comfortably, beginning then to writhe against him in more controlled, evenly paced and what she thought were seductive movements of her hips and groin.

It was at that moment Parrish balked. He had been all but raped yet knew that the fault was partly his. He knew of Lorraine's growing desires but did nothing to curtail them. Perhaps he had let them run their course for personal gratification or to see just what was beneath the woman's veneer of upper class respectability and quite how far she would go. Well now he knew, but had let it go too far. He knew she didn't want him personally. It was just animal lust and now, as he lay on his back watching Lorraine riding him with slow deliberation, almost sanctimonious in her control over him and the blatant display of what she knew was her beautiful body, he realized she was trying to be seductive, sensual and overall controlling of his rise to orgasm.

Just like Juli.

But what Juli made so beautiful, Lorraine turned repulsive.

And he was coercing with this woman. The sudden realization of his own degradation cut deeper than any dagger. Had living in this modern world corrupted him so much? So much that he would lay back and let events overtake him without so much as even token resistance?

Parrish’s sinking sense of what was right re-surfaced then like a breaching whale as the shock of truth brought him back to his senses. It was a stinging emotional slap in the face. He wasn't being made love to, as only Juli could, he was being fucked in mockery to the feelings he had shared with her.

Parrish’s anger rose like bile within him but, as he had learned through hard lessons as Chieftain of Danebury, he controlled it. With one great thrust of his hips, he threw Lorraine off and she rolled to one side, shock showing bold on her face as she slid off the edge of the bed to land with a thump on the floor, face down. Parrish was on the floor behind her in an instant, intent on turning the tables and ready to dish out some of what he had been taking. Gripping her hips he jerked her up into a kneeling position, pulling her onto all fours.

Kneeling between her legs he moved close and drove in with his hips, pushing hard into her wetness. She took his attack with a gasp with pleasure and, oblivious to Parrish's gritted teeth and hard expression, gratefully accepted his thrusts and quickly matched his rhythm.

It was harsh and fast now, yet the violence of it was lost to Lorraine and in moments she peaked again with another great shriek while Parrish didn't even break stride, wanting the affair to be over as soon as possible. Even so Lorraine still managed a third orgasm at the same moment she took Parrish's seed.

There was no satisfaction at all for him and what pleasure waves there were he rode with no more than a grunt.

Barely had he finished pulsing than he withdrew, looking down in distaste at Lorraine's glistening wetness upon him. She in contrast let out a long satisfied sigh and sank exhausted to the floor, laying before him in naked, sweating and sated abandonment.

Parrish rose quietly to his feet and looked down in disgust at the sprawling example of decadent humanity below him. She was totally unaware and uncaring about any consequences of her actions as long as her personal satisfaction was attained.

Without a word, the Chieftain of Danebury turned his back and walked away. He was headed towards the shower, urgently intent on washing off himself the unwanted residue of the twentieth century. But he felt so dirty he doubted any amount of showers would be enough to get the job done.

And for the first time since he could remember, he felt like crying.

16

There was a change in the air. Chris could feel it. He didn't know why and he wasn't about to ask, but something was either just about to happen, had recently happened, or maybe even both.

When he'd arrived home in the late afternoon he found Parrish just sitting in silence in the lounge, apparently deep in thought. Lorraine seemed almost unnaturally cheery while his usually indomitable friend was uncharacteristically sullen.

Lorraine cooked a meal for the three of them without a single word of protest and they sat at the table and ate in virtual silence while Chris was aware of his wife subtly trying to catch Parrish's eye but without success. It was as the meal came to an end when Parrish finally spoke.

"Tell me about the man who won all the money betting on the weather." He said straight out of the blue.

"Huh?" Chris grunted in surprise, verbally echoing the puzzlement on Lorraine's face.

"The man that bet on the weather." Parrish repeated. "What do you know about him?"

There was a brief moment of silence before husband and wife recalled the event at the same moment.

"Oh yes." It was Lorraine, eager to please now it seemed. "I remember now, don't you Chris? When we had that bad spell of unusual weather, just a few days before Shaun arrived."

Its Shaun now is it?, thought Chris as she continued.

"And this man appeared to have predicted the whole thing. He bet on it happening and made a bit of a killing from a number of betting shops. I believe it came to several hundred thousand pounds in total. Now, what was his name?"

"Clouder." Chris nodded. " In fact, I think we may still have the newspapers for that week out back. It was plastered all over them." He pushed himself away from the table. "I'll have a look." With that he left the room, going out to the utility room at the back of the house where Lorraine made him store all the items that could be recycled, including the daily papers.

Meanwhile Parrish had no intention of being alone with Lorraine any longer than was absolutely necessary. He too rose and went into the lounge. She followed and to prevent any pressing conversation from her he switched on the TV as he passed it then sat in the chair farthest from the sofa where she normally sprawled. The sound and vision came quickly up and he pretended to watch while keeping one eye on her. She just smiled gently back at him, biding her time, it seemed. In an odd way Parrish suddenly felt as if he were being stalked.

Moments later Chris reappeared and sat down between the two, a rather crumpled newspaper in his hands. After smoothing it out across his lap he held it out to Parrish, the astounding gambling coup boldly making the front page, the bulk of the face of the tabloid one huge colour picture of a man looking directly into the lens and holding aloft a betting slip.

The banner headline above it read:

WEATHER BET BRINGS STORM OF WEALTH TO LOCAL MAN

Parrish studied the face in the picture. The man didn't look particularly big or powerful, although the Chieftain of Danebury knew full well power came in many different guises. In fact the man gazing rather unemotionally out of the photograph seemed rather bookish. But of course, this was a man of brain not brawn, he could see it in the face, the eyes. Eyes that seemed to be smirking at the world. Eyes with a secret knowledge of some great power hidden there. This man knew many things. A knowledge and power that needed to be protected. No wonder he had hired Mister Tench. Parrish looked hard at the face. The face of his enemy.

Unaware of all this registering in Parrish's eyes, Chris pulled the paper away, settled back in his chair and read out loud, curious that his friend hung almost hungrily on each and every word.

“With an uncanny and incredible display of accuracy reminiscent of the prophet Nostradamus, the appropriately named Mister Paul Cloudier, Professor of languages at Southampton University, had predicted almost to the hour a number of what can only be described as highly unusual weather occurrences.

In three separate incidents it seems he foresaw a remarkable single monsoon type downpour, a record breaking thunderstorm and, most spectacularly of all, an incredible electrical storm which, although centered over the downs north of Stockbridge, struck several homes and farm buildings causing structural damage to a number of properties but thankfully no reported injuries."

Chris paused and glanced towards Parrish as if waiting for permission to carry on. Or had he already heard enough?

The man in question seemed to be mentally chewing over the words and there was a long pause before he said simply.

“Does it say where he lives?"

Chris's eyes fell back to the page and he quickly scanned the printed columns.

Lorraine's eyes never left Parrish but now there was no look of desire or secret knowledge of their earlier collusion. She too was engrossed with the mysterious reason as to why her sexual wild man was suddenly so deeply intrigued with this 'weather man' and his crass, money grabbing bets.

“Ah, here we are.” Chris held a finger to the pertinent area of text. "Mister Cloudier gave a brief statement outside his new home before retiring to the house and has since admitted no visitors and been seen by no one. His residence, Mile End House, between Romsey and Ampfield is a secluded building set in five acres of wooded grounds surrounded by a high wall. It was purchased only a few days earlier with we believe some of his new found wealth and we can exclusively reveal that the total cost of the property was well over two hundred thousand pounds!”

Chris's eyebrows shot up at the amount.

“I think I can find it." was all Parrish said, in a flat tone.

"You're going to try and see this man?" asked Lorraine. Parrish just cocked his head and glanced at her. She shook her head. "It'll just be a waste of time. It seems to me he has the intention of not letting anyone near him."

“Oh, I'll get near him all right."

"Yes, but why?" asked Chris. "Why go and see him in the first place?"

Parrish opened his mouth to reply but was stopped by a sudden gasp from Lorraine.

Both men looked to see her fumbling for the TV remote, her eyes not leaving the screen. With a stab of her finger the sound came up to a more audible level as all three looked at the image before them.

A rough likeness of Parrish in a line drawing loomed large on the screen for several moments before cutting to a place Parrish immediately recognized. It seemed somehow even more stark in the harsh light of the day but the view was unmistakably the side alley of Shadow casino. Although the alley ends were cordoned off with yellow tape and beat bobbies standing sentry, the cameraman still managed a good zoom shot of the blood splashed tarmac before next showing covered bodies being loaded into a waiting ambulance.

This was obviously a high profile Police investigation if this kind of footage, filmed earlier in the day, was being shown on the teatime news, along with the artists impression of the alleged attacker. As the almost too handsome news reporter stepped in front of the camera, skillfully blocking out the bulk of the grim scene to make the viewers focus solely on him, Parrish slumped back in his chair, almost physically feeling a net starting to close in around him.

Completely unaffected by the gruesome spectacle going on around him the reporter looked squarely into the eyes of the viewers through the camera lens, his voice full of gravity.

"With a brutality never before witnessed by the officers investigating this heinous crime, two apparently innocent passersby were savagely murdered by a lone attacker in the early hours of this morning. Although no one actually heard or saw the fatal incident, reliable witnesses have placed a man at the crime scene shortly before. The face you just saw was that man and the Police urgently need to speak to ..., ah, here is Detective Inspector Litten, the man leading this investigation."

A serious looking middle aged man of medium height with strong features and glittering, intelligent eyes was pulled into shot by the reporter. He eyed the man for a moment, letting him know he didn't like to be manhandled. The reporter looked momentarily uncomfortable at the wordless rebuke before quickly recovering and plunging into his well-rehearsed questions.

"Inspector, just how savage was this apparently unprovoked attack, what kind of a man could do such a thing, and just how soon will it be before the public can expect an arrest?"

Parrish thought the questions remarkably stupid. So did the Inspector and it showed in his face. If it weren't for the fact that this man was now hunting Parrish, he felt he might have actually liked him.

Inspector Latten let the asinine remarks go without censure. He knew what the public wanted and also knew how to work it to his own advantage.

"Well, Peter," His simple use of the man's name still managed to convey a hint of contempt, "This was a very brutal attack indeed. The second killing was carried out with such ferocity that part of the weapon is still I am told lodged inside the victim, no doubt broken off during the attackers frenzy."

The reported struggled to hide the glee in his eyes as he thrust the microphone ever more intently into the face of the Inspector. This was better than he could have hoped for. Extensive coverage of such a shocking incident and high profile investigation could really put him on the map of public perception.

The Inspector gazed directly into the lens then and spoke quietly but with great authority.

“The man who did this is without doubt a very cold, calculating and totally ruthless person. If anyone does see this person do not, I repeat do not attempt to approach him. Contact us immediately and keep well out of his way. He is clearly extremely dangerous and could easily kill again if even slightly provoked. We want him apprehended and removed from the public domain as quickly and quietly as possible."

“Thank you Inspector." Peter snatched the mike away and spun to face the camera once again, the camera man skillfully zooming in just enough to cut Inspector Latten completely from the shot. "To that end the owners of Shadow casino have, in the interest of public safety, offered a ten thousand pound reward for information that leads to the capture of the person or persons who inflicted this terrible crime on their premises. Here once again is that artists picture of the man the police wish to find in connection with this bloody and savage double murder. They have issued a contact number for anyone who might have information that would help with their enquiries. That number is ..."

The screen once more cut to the rather good likeness of Parrish but he never looked, turning as he felt the eyes of Chris and Lorraine on him.

"It's not like they say." he said rather lamely. "Those two men were going to kill me. I simply defended myself."

There was wide confusion on Chris's face. He believed his friend if he said it was self-defense, but to actually *kill* two men out in the street! That just wasn't like the Parrish he knew of old.

Lorraine simply stared across at Parrish. Now past the erotic thrill of wild sex with a killer, she now felt a cold shock at the actual event. The image of that bleak alley stayed with her. The place where there had been a cold, blood splattered murder of two human beings, carried out by the man now sitting opposite her.

There was a silence, broken only by the unheeded voices from the TV, before Chris looked down at his hands, still clutching the forgotten newspaper, and said quietly.

“What you gonna do now?"

“They'll be looking for me. All they need now is a starting place. Then it'll just be a matter of time."

At that moment, as if fate had conspired to make a bad situation worse, the very next news report was a rehash of the museum theft in Devizes. A mysterious crime with no apparent motive, the theft of a virtually worthless piece of stone. There were no obvious leads at this time.

Parrish looked on in dismay. He could almost see Bob out there somewhere, diving for the telephone to tell the police just where he had picked up and dropped off a man who fitted the description shown only moments earlier. And also happy of course to hold out his hand for the ten thousand pound bounty.

Parrish was glad he'd at least had the presence of mind to meet Bob's taxi away from the house itself. It had probably bought him a few hours but in no time at all the police would be swarming all over this area of the city. The decision had been made for him.

"I must leave." he said. "As soon as it's dark."

He rose to his feet, waited for a moment for words that he knew would never come, then said quietly, "I'd better sort out my kit." and left the stunned pair to their silence.

There wasn't much at all to check out and the Chieftain of Danebury sat in silence in the middle of the bedroom floor, brooding. Apart from sorting through all the effects he kept in his jacket pockets, cleaning his new boots and donning his dark jeans and a black polo neck to help him hide in the night, he could do no more than wait for the darkness to come.

The waiting itself came easy to him. It had once been said that he could out wait a stone. But the slow time forced him to look ahead. And to see his struggle against the constricting oppressions of the modern times. They pushed down on the freedom, honesty and downright straight forwardness that he so greatly missed from his time now long lost in the ancient past. He realized that the prospect of being trapped in the twentieth century was becoming more and more difficult to face. Especially now he was a hunted man. There would be nothing to look forward to once his mission was accomplished. Nothing but eventual capture and incarceration. That thought alone was totally repulsive to him. Even more so because in his own eyes he had done no wrong. It all began to frighten him.

Finally, the soft evening light melted away as the night crept in to blanket the land in its dark warmth.

It was time. His military training told him so, and that same training also spoke to Chris Dunn. As Parrish was pulling on his jacket there was a soft knock at the door and Chris slipped in, closing it quietly behind him.

Each looked at the other, both knowing this would be a final parting.

Parrish stepped forward and gripped his friend’s hand.

“Thanks Chris. Thanks for everything."

“It was nothing.” Chris shrugged with that typical modesty he always displayed when being praised.

"No. You've done a hell of a lot and I know that I might now have put you and your wife in the firing line. Here."

Releasing his grip he reached into his pocket and produced Klud's flint headed dagger. Chris took the strange gift without speaking and examined it as lay in his palm, a puzzled frown on his face.

"Give it a good while before you do anything with it." Parrish said quietly, "But when the time comes and you're alone, have that dated by a museum or University. They'll find it to be very old and an extremely rare example, being in such a good condition. If the collection I saw in Devizes is anything to go by, the British Museum should pay you handsomely for it.

“Er ... thanks." was all Chris could say, not for the first time finding it difficult to totally believe everything his old friend said.

“Parrish just smiled, glad that his good friend had missed the true reference to his eventually being alone. He was a shrewd enough judge of character to know that sooner rather than later, in no small part due to his own actions with Lorraine, Chris's wife would leave him. And not just leave him but, considering it all to be hers, take everything he had too. Without knowing it Chris held a fifty thousand pound insurance policy in his hand in the form of Klud's Neolithic ten-a-penny dagger.

“Just remember what I said.” Parrish patted the knife almost affectionately then moved passed Chris and left the room.

Chris dumbly followed and together they walked down to the front door, a heavy silence squeezing against them as the moment to leave swiftly approached.

Lorraine appeared in the lounge doorway and looked on without a word, a mixture of loss and relief entwined on her beautiful face as she too knew.

Parrish could feel no compassion for her. She had taken his body, taken Chris for a fool and would eventually take everything the man had, including his heart, just as her own mercenary instincts would take command the day she left. But he knew it was not all her fault. She was after all q product of the materialistic, fortune hunting and self-serving twentieth century.

He nodded at her, as much in acknowledgment of his understanding of the situation as in farewell, and she saw the nod for what it really was. Her expression hardened. The only thing she wanted now was to see him gone from her house. Parrish turned one last time to his friend and again gripped his hand.

"So long mate." he said quietly.

There was a sudden sheen in Chris's eyes and Parrish watched with great affection as his friend swallowed the lump in his throat. Their grips tightened for a moment, untold words of best wishes passing between them, before Chris let his hand drop.

"Watch your back." was all he said and switched off the hall light, plunging them into shadow, the only illumination then the indirect lighting coming from the lounge behind Lorraine.

It was the gesture of one professional to another, a man trying to make a situation as safe as possible for his oppo.

Parrish just turned and slipped silently out into the night and heard the door click softly shut behind him. After a brief pause to check that the area was clear he sprinted across the road and into the strip of woodland that marked the edge of the golf course, at the same time swallowing the lump in his own throat.

17

The Chieftain of Danebury crossed the open areas of the golf course as quickly but as quietly as he could before plunging into the inky blackness of the Forestry Commission land that butted against its northern boundary.

This densely wooded area, stretching right to the edge of the M27 motorway that swept around the northern limit of the city, was almost all crop grown pinewoods. Nothing grew beneath the thick evergreen foliage which blanked out virtually all the ambient light, keeping the forest floor in dark shadow even on the brightest of days. At night the pine needle covered ground was swathed in almost impenetrable blackness and Parrish gladly wrapped it around him like a child's security blanket. After his dash across the open he dove straight into the pines, running on perhaps another fifty or so yards before going to ground to regain his breath and check for any possible pursuers.

It was a warm enough night and as Parrish waited there was something comforting about being back in a wilderness, no matter how small it might be, and being away from the stifle of people. He sat with his back against a tree, the heady pine smell filling his senses, and let the calmness flow into him, becoming like any other creature of the woods. Still but alert, eyes and ears open to anything and everything, waiting. A waiting time that is beyond any clock. That sort of time cannot be measured. The creatures and plants simply wait until the time is right to do what has to be done. Subconsciously, Dannu's man understood this.

From a little way off, at the other end of the enclosure he

now occupied, there came a single cough of a fox, out on the prowl. Then Parrish felt something on his hand. He had to lift his fist to within a few inches of his face to see the lone wood ant that crawled there. He couldn't help it. A smile came to his face and it seemed like the first one in a long while.

Time to move on.

It was slow going but Parrish felt safe and in no need to hurry. He felt his way across the uneven, springy forest floor treading gently with his boots and with hands outstretched to ward off any unseen low branches. It was natural to him now that he moved with very little sound and after a while his ears began to pick up the distant roar of the motorway ahead of him.

Then the light from it began to filter through the darkness. He recalled that part of the highway, either side of the Rownhams services, being an illuminated section and began to home in on the light like a moth. Creeping up to the boundary fence he gazed across at the fat ribbon of tarmac, alive with vehicles of every description flashing past in both directions and vanishing from sight in only a few seconds. It wasn't just their speed that amazed him but the sheer volume of traffic at this time of night. Didn't anyone sleep in this modern world? Even though he knew it to be the early hours of the morning the traffic was virtually constant and he decided against trying to dash straight across six high speed lanes. From his stationary view point the idea seemed almost suicidal.

He tracked along the tree line until it drew level with the rear boundary of the south side services area. This pit stop for the motorist was also quite busy and Parrish had to wait a few minutes before there was a lull. He quickly clambered over the wire then strolled boldly across the well lit car park, heading straight for the main buildings just as if he had only moments before parked up and was going in for a cuppa. Luckily the access way to the foot bridge that linked the two sides of the service areas was just inside the foyer and Parrish didn't have to run the gauntlet of a bustling restaurant and shopping arcade.

It was of course unavoidable that he would encounter other members of the public and that hunted feeling fell heavily back across him. Yet no one seemed to appear remotely interested in him and he crossed the footbridge, descended to the north side foyer and ducked back out into the open as quickly as he could without outwardly appearing to hurry.

This car park was a mirror image of the first and once again he strode manfully away across it heading towards his non-existent car, until inevitably there were no more vehicles between him and the boundary fence. Beyond was another enclosure of pinewood. Only then did he break into a run, vault the wire and dash into the leafy darkness without looking back.

If he had checked his trail he might have seen the man who sat motionless in his car, watching in frozen recognition as Parrish passed close by his vehicle before vanishing into the night. With a hand that trembled partly in realization of his narrow escape from a mad kilter and partly in anticipation of a chance at a well publicized large reward, the man reached for his mobile phone.

Parrish continued to travel northward at his measured pace and passed by the hamlet of Toothill then crossed the open farmland behind North Baddesley with an ever growing confidence now he didn't appear to be public enemy number one. Ahead of him was an expanse of mixed woodland that occupied almost a square kilometer of ground. It was just a dark smudge on the night horizon but he knew it hid from his sight the lights of Whitenapp on the edge of Romsey. Only a few miles beyond that lay Ampfield and his intended destination, Mile End House.

But the dawn was now drawing ever nearer. Parrish decided to get a few hours rest in the woods and perhaps try his luck around the edge of Romsey during the next day if the streets weren't too busy. A short while later he crossed a single track tarmaced lane then entered the wood immediately noting the change to deciduous trees, more by their different scents than by sight. It was a refreshing change after several hours in the pinewoods. The forest floor was also covered in a good growth here, very high in some places although bare in the open glades where it appeared animals had roamed and grazed.

Settling deep under a leafy bush he allowed himself to relax and tried to sleep, only then realizing just how tired he felt. There was no doubting his fitness but the last two days had been particularly stressful and it did not take long before he slipped away into a restful sleep.

The warmth of the sun on his face finally roused him. He squinted, rubbed the sleep from his face then gazed up through the leafy canopy at the hot orb. It was high in the sky. High enough to be nearly midday he realized with surprise, and it looked like there was another fine day in the offing and he had already missed half of it. Still, no matter, the sleep had done him good and he felt greatly refreshed.

Rising to his feet Parrish drew in a few deep breaths while enjoying a good stretch before briefly brushing small pieces of forest debris from his clothes then setting off once more, aware of the emptiness in his stomach but not in the least bothered by it. It wasn't the first time he had gone more than twelve hours without food.

With an air of quiet determination about him he moved on through the trees, taking his bearings from the warm sun and heading still northwards towards the woodland edge and the border of Romsey.

Just as he was thinking that things were moving smoothly along and definitely going his way, he emerged from the tree line and stood stock still. Only a few hundred yards in front of him was a straggling line of parked police vehicles with a large number of uniformed men milling apparently aimlessly around between them.

“There he is!" went up a cry and all the faces turned in his direction, a few men beginning to run towards him.

Parrish just turned like a startled deer and bolted straight back into the trees, trying to ward off the sudden shock and think how he might avoid immediate capture. But thankfully he heard his pursuers immediately called off by a commanding voice on a bull horn.

Stand fast!" It bellowed. "He won't get far and we'll catch him soon enough on the sweep."

Now out of their sight Parrish didn't stop, thinking on the run. He recognized the loud-hailer voice as the policeman from the TV. Detective Inspector Litten. And he also recognized the implication of the extra information about the forthcoming sweep, tacked almost carelessly onto the end of the announcement. There's no point in trying to escape, it said. Save us all a lot of bother and just give yourself up. Parrish scoffed at the insult of it. He was Chieftain of Danebury and the warriors of that village did not just give up. If they thought this man hunt was going to be easy they had better think again.

It took a few minutes at the run for the Danebury man to reach the southern edge of the woods, not far from where he had entered the night before. The lane there was also occupied by a number of police vehicles. Not half as many as on the north side, which at once told Parrish which side the sweep would start from, but still enough to hem him neatly in. He didn't rate his chances of sneaking through the line either. One of the vehicles he instantly recognized as an armed response unit. He might outrun a man but not a bullet.

On reflection the north group didn't look as if they were about ready to start the sweep yet, so he still had a little time. Even though he could almost physically feel the pressure of the hunt and trepidation at the prospect of capture and what that would mean, he couldn't help but admire Litten. It didn't matter how Parrish had been found but plainly the Inspector could move fast when needed and organize large numbers of men quickly too. Clearly the man had the makings of a good Chieftain in him.

But now it was Parrish who had to move fast. There was no escape and he wasn't about to give himself up. He must hide.

Moving back towards the north end of the woods but making sure he kept well out of sight of the police he quickly chose his spot. An open area, which the searchers would not pay such keen attention to as it would immediately appear to be empty, but still with enough floor cover for him to burrow under.

At the edge of the open glade stood a sprawling oak, with a partially visible root system, that had scattered the ground beneath its arms with last year's leaves. They had all turned to a fine mulch which was as much a part of the woodland floor as the grasses, tufts of bracken and low plants that grew through it. Working quickly, he began to dig himself what amounted to a shallow grave, with the space for his head in the vee of two roots and the length of his body effectively laid out in the open. Carefully piling the forest debris that covered the topsoil along one side of the trench, he began to scoop out the rich earth, heaping it into his spread out jacket before carrying each load away into the woods where he slung it into a bush. If the spoil were discovered, which it most likely would be, it would become an added distraction.

The job didn't take too long. The soil didn't even need breaking up, it was so loamy. Using a recently fallen bough that still had most of its foliage Parrish bunched it tightly up into a tiny briar that would just cover where his head would lay so he could see a little and have a breathing hole. Then he tried his 'grave' out for size, checking that he had enough mulch to cover himself and the leg end was deep enough for his boots not to stick up and give his position away. When he was satisfied he moved as close as he dare to the edge of the woods and watched the final preparations being made before the search started. Those under his watchful gaze seemed to be in no immediate hurry. Perhaps Litten was trying to make him sweat? Well he was succeeding! At least there appeared to be only a few dogs and Parrish hoped the smell of the freshly dug soil would mask his scent

The hole in the ground was crude work but it was the best he could do. The idea was that once the searchers had formed a line and started to move in he would bury himself, wait until the search line had passed by then make good his escape. The Army escape and evasion instructors made it all sound so simple. Parrish was about to put it to the test.

It was time.

Parrish saw Litten talk briefly into a walkie-talkie, no doubt a last minute check to see if his target had been caught by the perimeter guards. Then with a broad flourish of his arm the line of uniforms, now armed with long sticks to beat the bushes, night sticks to protect themselves and with a small number of dogs spaced evenly along the line, moved in an orderly fashion towards the edge of the woods.

The man they were so intent on finding slipped back to his oak glade and sat down in his grave. He carefully spread mulch over his feet, legs and lap before laying back, draping his combat jacket across his upper torso and covering that too. With his one uncovered arm he pushed mulch up over his neck and around his head before positioning the briar to mask his face. Then he burrowed the arm under the mulch by his side, doing his best to leave the ground as undisturbed looking as possible. He'd now daren't move his head and could only look straight up. His view was blocked there by the tight knit of the briar bunch but peripheral vision allowed him to see movement if it were very close. Doing his best to suppress the tension and turmoil within him he tried to concentrate on keeping his breathing shallow and silent.

The line of searchers drew nearer. Parrish could hear the slow approach of their sticks as they beat on the ground and thrashed the bushes, the occasional voice and the more distant pant and growl of dogs straining at the leash.

Just then a light breeze blew into the woods, developing in a few seconds to a strong gust. It whooshed through the trees, bending the small branches and disturbing the ground cover, swirling energetically into Parrish's glade. Lots of loose debris, leaves, small twigs and dried bracken were caught in the turbulence and swept across the open glade towards the spreading oak beneath which he lay.

The broad bulk of the tree's trunk seemed to break up the airflow and the swirling wind instantly lost its strength, depositing all the airborne debris it carried on the ground in front of it, covering in moments the unnatural looking man shaped hump on the ground there. The wind died and was gone in seconds, the previously fresh bulges in the ground now indistinguishable from any other undulation on the floor of the glade.

"God! That whipped up a bit sudden." came an abrupt voice immediately beside the oak, close on Parrish's left side.

"Yes." A slightly higher pitched tone than the first voice, this one coming from almost beside Parrish, on his right. A stick thumped the ground beside his head. "One of those dust devils they call dervishes in foreign countries. Like a baby tornado. What you would call a localized weather phenomenon. Happens if the wind is in the right direction."

"Bugger 'weather phenomenon'," cursed the first voice. "It blew dust and shit everywhere. I've got summat in my eye."

The man rubbed his eyes with both hands, dropping his stick in the process. It landed across Parrish's legs.

"Try pulling your top lid over the bottom one. That usually works."

The first man did as instructed and gave an instant sigh of relief.

"Hey, you're right. Still can't she shit though, their watering like anything."

He picked up his stick and Parrish got a glimpse of the man as he leant into his field of vision. A young, fresh faced constable, perhaps not fully understanding what he was supposed to be doing or quite how to do it.

"Yes, well it'll sort itself out in a minute. C'mon, better keep up with the rest of the line or Litten will go ballistic. You know how he likes to keep things organized and orderly."

The pair laughed in agreement, turned their gaze to the far side of the glade and moved quickly across the open space, one of them inadvertently clipping the barely covered toe of Parrish's boot with his own as he went.

A moment later they were gone, the only sound in the glade then the soft whoosh as Parrish let out the burning breath he'd been holding all that time

18

Like a young shoot, newborn from the soil, Parrish emerged slowly, tentatively from the ground. Just his head at first then, after checking that the glade was clear, he climbed out.

The symbolism was lost on the man though. His concentration was fully on making good his escape. It would not do just to run blindly away for he had his mission. He needed transport now.

Absently brushing clinging bits of humus from himself he donned his jacket then moved smartly off to the north, eyes and ears alert for the merest hint of discovery. It didn't come. All he could hear was the search line moving steadily away behind him.

Coming once again to the edge of the wood he scanned the vehicles ahead. Two constables stood guard over them, talking together beside a large box wagon at one end of the row. Parrish knew well enough why they were there. Partly because the van was a carbon copy of the other armed response vehicle he'd seen earlier and there was kudos to be had by just being seen in its vicinity. Secondly they wished to stay well clear of the man who sat alone in the big saloon car at the other end of the row. A man of authority.

The Danebury man watched for a few minutes, aware of the precious time ticking away but waiting for the right moment. It arrived when one of the constables produced a packet of cigarettes from his pocket and the other gathered in next to him to gain a light. Parrish moved in.

Inspector Litten was taking occasional progress reports of

the search on his walkie-talkie and plotting them with a soft lead pencil onto the large scale map spread across his lap. He was briefly aware of a sudden movement beside the car then his door was snatched violently open. Before he knew what had happened he found himself flat on the ground beside the vehicle, face down.

There was an arm locked about his throat, a knee jammed into his back and a hand across his forehead, pulling his head roughly back. He was sharply aware of a strong earth smell. Choking against the arm that was pressuring his windpipe he tried to struggle. This only increased the pressure. He stopped, fighting against the desperate urge to break free, and lay very still.

“Wh ... what ..?” he gasped.

“Keys!" hissed a low but very insistent voice.

Litten didn't answer straight away and Parrish gave his neck another persuasive squeeze.

"Keys." he repeated.

“In the ignition.” croaked Litten struggling vainly for breath. As reward for the correct answer Parrish relaxed some of his grip. He leaned in close and spoke softly into the man’s ear.

“I'm not the mad killer you make me out to be. Those two men were going to kill me. I just defended myself.” He wasn't quite sure why he was explaining his actions to Litten but it somehow made him feel better.

Litten knew his time had come. Yet Parrish had been right in his earlier judgment of the man, the Inspector was a man of conviction. His whole life had been built on the principles of right and wrong. That's why he was a good, honest policeman. He would not beg for his life but he would not absolve this man of his crimes, even to save himself. He said what he thought.

"You still killed them. Slaughtered them. That makes you a murderer."

"Then by rights I should kill you too." hissed Parrish angrily. “Remember that."

He locked his arm hard around Litten's throat. The Inspector gasped but no breath came. He started to kick and struggle but it was futile. There was no strength in him. Panic rose hard in his chest. He tried to summon up his last reserves of strength but everything blurred, the blood roared in his ears and he lapsed into unconsciousness.

Immediately the man beneath him went limp Parish jumped off and turned him over. Checking that he was merely out for the count he put him gently into the recovery position.

The two policemen at the far end of the row had seen nothing, the whole incident hidden behind the car Parrish now climbed into. He took a brief moment to re-familiarize himself with the controls then turned the key. The motor roared instantly to life. The bobbies looked curiously up as Parrish selected first then gave the car the gun, flashing past the open mouthed men even before they could reach for their own radios.

Because Litten's car was unmarked only the police would immediately recognize it and this Parrish hoped would give him the time he needed. After clearing the edge of the wood, he took the vehicle along the country lanes, for a moment forgetting his hunters and whatever lay ahead, just reveling in the thrill of once again travelling at speed. With the window wound fully down he thrust first his arm and then his face into the slipstream and laughed out loud to feel the push of the air against him. But even this modern joy was short lived.

He came to a junction with a more major road. The sign opposite read.

A3057 Romsey 1 mile.

Parrish took the turn carefully and was soon joined with the light traffic heading into the market town.

Once more the hunted look came upon him, as if every eye was turned searchingly in his direction, doubly so now that he was at the wheel of a stolen car. And yet again no one saw a thing. He was just one more innocuous car with a faceless driver in the constant flow of vehicles.

Making sure to keep pace with this flow so as to blend in Parrish drove into Romsey, smoothly negotiated a small roundabout at the edge of the town and took the turn indicating Ampfield, Hursley and Winchester.

He recalled this particular road and drove confidently back out of the suburbs and into the countryside. Barely a mile further along this route lay a length of arrow straight road, just one section of the A3090 according to the map but known to all locally as the straight mile. Parrish began to slow and scanned left and right for a sign or name plate.

A few vehicles overtook him as he searched but he ignored them. Still no sign. In little over a minute he had just about reached the end of the straight mile and began to fear that he had somehow missed what he sought, but just where the road began to curve away towards the next village he saw it. A short, graveled spur road no more than ten or fifteen meters long led off to a tall pair of black wrought iron gates. The slate panel high up on the right hand pillar was plain enough.

Mile End House.

Parrish drove straight onto the spur and braked carefully to a stop, nosing the car up till it was almost touching the gates. After all the recent news coverage he half expected camera crews and reporters but the area appeared deserted. He climbed out, went to the gates and briefly eyed the fat, shiny new padlock clasping the two together, before gazing up at the building beyond. It was set in the middle of neatly manicured lawns with shrubs and bushes along the borders, the whole place encircled by its high Victorian wall.

The gravel track led straight on to the front of the house, ending in a turn around. The building itself was well over a hundred years old, tall and quite elegant with steeply pitched roofs, lofty brick chimneys, big square sliding sash windows and a short flight of steps up to the front entrance.

From above, in the broad trunked beech trees that towered up over both the main gates and Parrish, came a sudden loud cawing and he looked up to see a small rookery lodged among the high branches. This was the place all right.

He moved aside, clambered over the wall, dropped lightly into the garden and walked slowly up towards the house, taking care to stay off the noisy gravel until he had to cross the turn around. A single vehicle sat there and it was one he recognized. The BMW's bodywork had been repaired but the number plate was right. Without breaking stride Parrish climbed the steps, paused briefly to gauge just how sturdy the solid oak door was, then pounded firmly on it with the heavy iron knocker hanging at its center.

There was a bit of a wait but he didn't feel it necessary to knock a second time. It wasn't the kind of waiting of people in queues, more a motionless pause as if the world briefly held its breath at the edge of a special moment.

Almost abruptly the door swung back and to Parrish's surprise the man himself stood framed in the doorway.

Parrish was momentarily lost for words

"I don't know your name, but I know who you are." said Professor Clouder by way of introduction. "Won't you come in?"

Parrish hesitated briefly. He wasn't afraid, just unsure about what might happen next. But this man seemed amicable and reasonable enough on first impression. Besides, he was Chieftain of Danebury and it was he who should be bold and stamp his authority on the meeting. Nodding in acknowledgment he stepped assuredly into the building, yet acutely aware of the big oak door being shut firmly behind him. Then Clouder was with him.

"Here, let me take your coat."

Parrish obligingly shrugged out of his combat jacket and the professor hung it up before leading him down the spacious hallway towards a door on the right.

"Go on in, make yourself at home." he said almost too cheerily. "D'you know, I've been rather expecting you. I wasn't sure exactly when but I knew someone would come. It was only a matter of time."

The one sided banter appeared quite jovial but the serious undertones caused Parrish to shoot him a hard glance. The man sounded very reminiscent of the holy men of Dannu. Could he be that powerful?

The pair stopped in the center of a large lounge. The room appeared in no way sinister, being high roofed, light and airy with plate glass patio doors at one end. There were two sprawling leather sofas, a scattering of smaller pieces of furniture and opposite the door a wide mouthed Adams fireplace housing a real fire. With the trinkets on its mantelpiece and the brass tongs, poker and cleaning brush hanging beside the grate, the whole effect was of a quaint, homely feel. But that was the last thing Parrish felt as he heard the lounge door shut and turned to find a tall man with a good build standing easily in front of it. Blocking it.

"Don't be afraid." The professor spoke quickly on seeing Parrish tense, mistaking readiness for fear. "This is my friend Mister Tench."

The man at the door made no such error, recognizing Parrish's true response. Although he remained stone faced Parrish saw the understanding in his cold eyes. This man was a fighter. Even a warrior of sorts perhaps.

" I think we've met before." he said slowly, their eyes locked together.

At that Mister Tench smiled momentarily before the expression dropped from his face and it was as if he had never smiled in his life. And still he did not speak, just watched.

"Really?" Professor Clouder's eyebrows shot up but he didn't dwell on the subject. "Please, sit. We have much to discuss."

Parrish sank slowly, tightly controlled, onto the sofa nearest him and Clouder moved across and sat opposite. Parrish turned his attention to the smaller man who paused for a long moment before speaking.

"Now Mister ... er ... sorry, I'm afraid I don't know your name?"

Parrish was about to lift himself proudly, ready to announce himself as Chieftain but something told him to hold back. To not give any more information than was necessary.

"Parrish." he said curtly. "Shaun Parrish."

"Well, Mister Parrish, why exactly have you come to me, and at some peril to yourself I believe?"

Parrish let that remark pass too. Information like that could easily be gained simply by watching the TV.

"I've come to ask you to stop meddling." he said quietly.

"Meddling?"

"Yes. In things you don't understand." He wasn't fooled for a moment by the feigned expression of bafflement on Clouder's face. "You don't deny it was you who caused the changes in the weather?"

A soft smile came to Clouder's lips at that.

"Oh that was me all right. But that wasn't meddling my friend. That was just practice."

Parrish scoffed. "I think it was for the money."

"Oh no." Clouder sounded genuinely offended by the remark. "The money simply helped me find and fund this place. It's private, secluded and has an area perfect for me to take things further. Much further."

The man's eyes momentarily glanced downwards. Parrish

read the hastily disguised action but did not betray his understanding. A cellar.

"Further! You can't be serious?" said Parrish, shocked. “The weather's not something to be just mucked about with. And you're killing people. My people. Not here and now but it *is* happening."

Clouder just looked on disbelieving and it was his turn to scoff.

“I wasn't aware of any deaths, but that is of no concern to me. I intend to take this as far as I can."

Parrish just sat and stared at the professor. It was such a callous and careless remark and he saw it now. This small, bookish man had tasted it, liked it and wanted more. Power. So much for him appearing to be reasonable.

The Danebury man changed tack.

"So tell me. Just how did you discover this unusual ability?"

Clouder smiled broadly then and clasped his hands together in self congratulation. He felt in complete control and sitting opposite him was someone at last who might fully appreciate the time and effort that had gone into his research.

“I'm primarily a language professor," he explained. “and I've spent the last few years researching the ancient tongues of Britain and Europe. After a while, when I had built up a quite extensive data base, I began to notice similar words and phrases cropping up in several places, particularly in Roman Latin and on into Old English. And, more importantly, snippets of a past, Pagan religion. Much seemed to be made of it in the scraps of writings I found concerning the pre-Roman religion of Albion that had been passed on by the few scholars of Rome who were known to have visited these shores during the early days of occupation. Slowly I began to piece the bits together. At first it was hard enough just to de-code and understand the ancient tongue. Especially with the incomplete pieces of script I had. But I succeeded."

Parrish just nodded, letting the man rattle on in his growing excitement.

“Only then could I see the basis of the ancient religion and begin to understand it. No mean feat I'm sure you'll agree. That of course took me on to visit numerous museums to study the artifacts there. With this additional help I started to gain an appreciation of this virtually lost religion, get to grips with it and begin learning to control it."

“Of course, some museum pieces were necessary for you to start building a shrine of your own." Parrish said flatly.

Clouder's eyebrows shot up as he saw that the man before him really did know something of this old Earth religion. Perhaps even more than himself, although it was difficult to understand just how. Still, he saw the chance to advance his own knowledge. And power.

"Yes. It's coming along rather nicely, and with it more and more control." Parrish found it hard to hide his contempt.

"You only have that control because She is so weak here." he said. It was the first time he'd actually mentioned her but now was not the time to be evasive.

"You really *do* understand." Clouder said emphatically.

More than you will ever know, thought Parrish.

"Yes, but not why she hasn't stopped you from doing what you are doing."

This brought a self-satisfied smile to Clouder's face.

“She cannot. She is so weak now as to have all but completely lost her control. The bulk of her power came from the worship of her followers. But that was long, long ago. Now there are none and Nature goes its own sweet way.

Only myself, by understanding the rites and chants and harnessing what power is left in the ancient pieces of stone she used as conduits, only I have begun to unlock the immense potential. I alone have the power now. The power of Dannu has long since gone."

The mention of the Earth Goddess's real name by the man actually hurt Parrish. Clouder's flippant use of it sounded somehow blasphemous. Yet the Chieftain of Danebury, even in the face of such an insult, held himself in check. He needed more.

"But if you didn't disrupt the weather for money, and I believe you said it was for practice, then practice for what?"

"It was rather fun, actually." Clouder's eyes glittered with excitement. "But although I can now do certain things, it will take more time and understanding to do more. There is truly great potential there and it is now almost within my grasp. Learning to control the weather is but one step. Once I have learned to control all the basic elements, particularly water, I can do as I please." Urgency was thick in his voice now, his breathing was faster and a trace of spittle appeared in one corner of his mouth as he became more animated and thrilled by his own future prospects.

“Water?" asked Parrish, quite baffled at this latest revelation.

"Yes!" Clouder leaned forward and stared deep into Parrish’s eyes. Only then, as Parrish gazed unflinchingly back, did he see the small hint of madness lurking there. "Don't you see? People consist mostly of water!"

Parrish nodded as full understanding dawned then.

Once more Clouder misread the action as a final understanding of the full enormity of the power of Dannu. But Parrish was nodding in the final realization that this madman just had to be stopped. Not just prevented from going any further but stopped. Permanently. It wasn't a case of revenge for the abuse of Dannu and the misuse of her power. Or retribution for the lives lost back, millennia ago now, at Danebre. It was simply the decision of a warrior and Chieftain that this man was beyond help and so should be ritually killed. For his own good and everyone else's protection, for no one and nothing was safe while this man lived.

As the thoughts crossed Parrish’s mind Clouder sat slowly back and began to relax, gratified to explain all his efforts to someone who could fully appreciate them. And pleased too that he knew he was still in control for there was still a matter to be resolved. His voice was once more measured and controlled.

"As I used the power, I felt the Goddess's feeble attempts at rebellion but there was no strength left in her. I could read her thoughts." He looked smugly across at Parrish." I knew she would send someone. A last ditch attempt to wrest the power from me." He crossed his arms almost majestically across his puny chest. "But of course, you do know that that will never happen and all your efforts have been in vain?"

There were no more words to be said. No more options left to try.

Parrish simply nodded, his face a picture of dejection, defeat settling heavily on his shoulders. He slumped forward in his seat as if totally beaten, then suddenly launched himself at Clouder, springing across the gap between the two sofas. A look of utter terror froze on the man's face as Parrish pounced, reaching for the soft, white, unprotected throat.

Then Mister Tench was there.

19

A powerful blow to Parrish's unprotected ribs drove the wind from his body and sent him sideways, away from Clouder, and he bounced off the furthest arm of the sofa before crashing to the floor. Turning the fall into an awkward roll he twisted and came swiftly to his feet, fighting for a breath.

The Professor, recovered from his paroxysm of fear sprang from his seat as if scolded and darted behind the protective bulk of mister Tench. There was a frozen moment as the unlikely pair eyed Parrish and he stared straight back. Clouder was chilled to the core by the iciness of his attacker's glare and slowly, almost involuntarily, moved slowly back towards the lounge door.

"Tha ...thank you, Mister Tench." he gasped, the intent in Parrish's eye making him realize the true narrowness of his escape. And the wisdom of taking Mister Tench into his employ. The extortionate sum the man had asked for was suddenly worth every penny. He took several deep breaths to steady his nerve, pulled open the door and said slowly to his bodyguard, "You know what to do." Barely had the last word left his lips when he darted through the opening and slammed the door hard shut behind him.

Mister Tench smiled then. A smile of glee and menace. Of the joy of menace. Like an attack dog unleashed and finally happy to be at his work. He slowly began to advance on Parrish.

Parrish never waited for the man. He leapt to the attack, a pile driver right fist striking for the face while simultaneously jamming the fingers of his left hand into a tight cone and jabbing hard into his opponent's midriff.

Mister Tench's natural instinct overcame him at that moment and both hands came up to protect his face, skillfully deflecting away the aimed blow. But the lower attack struck home and he grunted in unexpected pain, the noise drawing some satisfaction from Parrish. But this man was fitter than Parrish had expected and the hit neither winded nor floored Mister Tench, he just staggered against it. Pressing home his early advantage Parrish moved smartly in and as the man dropped his guard he butted him in the face, the clash of heads opening up the big man's left eyebrow. It was this actual drawing of blood that seemed to galvanize Mister Tench as he reeled, a hand going to his face before inspecting it to see the bright red blood there.

Parrish continued to push home his attack intent on finishing the fight quickly. His Army training had taught him that in most violent encounters the first man to draw blood won out because of the instant psychological demoralization of the other.

Not so with Mister Tench. A cold grin came to his face as Parrish closed and the Danebury man suddenly found his own tactic used against him, Mister Tench leaping forward instead of reeling back. With blurring swiftness he punched Parrish left and right into the ribs, the blows stopping his advance, and followed up with a bone jarring forearm smash across the face that snapped Parrish's head to one side and spun him away. Now it was Mister Tench's turn to press home his attack with an agony producing rabbit punch to his opponents exposed lower back and kidney area.

Parrish gasped and involuntarily arched his back against the pain, unwittingly helping Mister Tench who grabbed him by the shoulder of his polo neck shirt and the waistband of his jeans, stepped up close beside him and with skillful use of leverage hurled Parrish clean over one sofa to crash forcibly against the wall beyond.

Somewhere in the back of his mind Parrish realized that he had come up against a man who had at least as much, if not more combat training than himself. But he could not dwell on it.

Staggering to his feet to find the man closing rapidly, Parrish right crossed him to the jaw. But Mister Tench simply rolled with the blow, taking the punch almost gladly. Did he actually enjoy the pain? Allowing Parrish to follow through after the blow, his arm going to full extension, Mister Tench drove in hard at the once again unprotected ribs. The single, power packed punch smashed home and Parrish felt at least one rib crack. There wasn't even time to react to that pain. His now frighteningly efficient attacker flowed smoothly in, wedged his shoulder into Parrish's armpit, gripped the still outstretched arm with both hands and with a deftly executed judo throw, hurled Parrish across the room again.

This time he smashed down on a glass and mahogany framed coffee table, crashing through it, the glass shards cutting into his back in several places. It was a struggle this time to rise and he knew he was too slow. He felt rather than saw the man close and it was all he could do to raise his hands in defense. To no effect.

Mister Tench, with perfect timing, waited until Parrish had just regained his feet then delivered a well aimed kick to the groin. The pain was so acute as to deny Parrish breath enough to scream. He clutched at his genitals, collapsed to the floor and curled gasping into a ball. But that was no protection either. He felt himself hauled roughly to his knees and his hair gripped in an iron fist that snapped his head roughly back. Through streaming tears of pain, he saw the glee on Mister Tench's face. That and the hand that drew back, stiff and knife edged, ready to chop down on his unprotected windpipe.

So this was it, was Parrish's only thought. After everything he had been through, this was how it all ended for him.

The blow fell but he did not die.

Instead of finishing him, the strike came not across his throat but down onto his cheekbone. Not quite hard enough to break it but with more than enough power to make Parrish's teeth clash together and the pain explode in his eye socket, fill his head and shoot down into his neck and arm. Through a red mist Parrish understood. Not only was this man a well trained and very skillful hand-to-hand fighter, probably an ex Para or maybe even SAS, he understood too just how much punishment a body could take. But when the moment for the killer strike had come he did not, would not take it. It wasn't enough for him to beat an opponent. This man liked to *beat* his opponents. He enjoyed inflicting the pain and Parrish realized with horror that it wasn't over yet.

The sadist hauled the sagging Parrish to his feet and, steadying him briefly with his left hand, drew back and punched him in the face hard enough to send him sprawling. Now both men had an open eyebrow, the blood running unnoticed down their cheeks. There was not even enough time to get to all fours before Mister Tench deftly kicked him hard in the spine making him fall back, writhing in pain on the carpeted floor. It was all he could do to turn onto his side, his back away from the man who bent over him, in an effort to protect his battered kidneys. This in no way deterred Mister Tench. With cold deliberation he leant slowly down and, using the karate technique of shaping his fist so that the first knuckle of his middle finger protruded, drove it hard into the meaty part of Parrish’s thigh. It was the hot, searing, soul deep pain of this spiteful blow that finally caused Parrish to shout out in agony. No playground 'dead leg' this but a brutally delivered piece of muscle damaging torture. The dreadful cry was what Mister Tench has sought and he took the time to savour it, giving out a triumphant laugh before punching again into the same spot.

The pain was so terrible that Parrish could not stop his second scream nor care who heard it either. He was beyond conscious thought then. A deep, instinctive drive rose within him. To get away, any way he could, from the pain. Away from the man inflicting the pain. With an almost superhuman effort he found a reserve of strength from somewhere and struggled to his feet, turning slowly, his arms lashing out hap-hazzardly in the hope of some lucky strike or just a chance to keep his attacker at bay.

With an undisguised laugh of vicious glee Mister Tench watched the semi recovery, realizing that there was still enough life in his victim to endure some more of his attentions. For a few moments he tortured Parrish by not hitting him, the hurt now in the fearful anticipation of the next attack. He began to circle the battered, bloody and swaying man, coolly picking out the next area on the body to assault. Sliding in under Parrish’s flailing arms he stalled his rotation by punching him again on his cracked ribs and, as the Danebury man gasped and leaned forward, drawing his arms in tight about his torso, slipped round behind him. His foot lashed out and the toe of his boot went hard into the back of Parrish's left knee. Both men heard the joint pop and the scream it produced was so high it was difficult to believe it came from the throat of a man. Parrish clutched at his knee and crashed to the floor again, the pain so intense he vomited.

Mister Tench took a few moments to savour this last blow and its effect. He understood how excruciatingly painful such an injury could be and that it would take several weeks for the swelling to go down and three times that for the ligaments heal. But then, it was his most favourite strike. Had anyone seen the great smile of total satisfaction on his face they would have been sickened by it. And there was more fun to be had yet, said the same expression.

Ignoring Parrish's retching, interspersed with racking pants of pain, he hauled him once again to his feet. The fact that Parrish could actually stand almost unaided meant the knee damage was not quite as extensive as had been intended. Taking a fresh grip on Parrish's polo neck and waist band, the cloth there slick with blood from the cuts in his back, Mister Tench hurled him across the room again, this time keeping his grip on the shirt. With a loud shredding rip the cloth was torn from Parrish's body and he hurtled bare-chested through the air, crashing into the Adams fireplace sending the brass ornaments flying.

Screaming afresh as the hot metal of the grate burned his bare flesh, he rolled back out onto the floor coming to rest face down among the trinkets and ornaments dislodged by his impact. He slowly drew his hands in till they were under his body, and just lay there gasping and sobbing in pain.

Mister Tench was just delighted. After tossing aside the shredded cloth he clapped his hands and laughed again before striding purposefully across and standing over the prostrate, bloodied and battered body. He bent slowly down into a half squat, his forearms resting on his thighs like a child inspecting some insect he had just discovered in the dirt. With an almost detached interest he examined the results of his handiwork, head nodding slowly in satisfaction. The excited glitter in his eyes was unmistakable, as was the perverse pleasure in his voice when he finally spoke.

"Time to die now." he whispered in a very matter-of-fact way.

With a groan Parrish rolled onto his back, and Mister Tench just had time to recognize the item in the clenched fists before the Chieftain of Danebury lunged upwards with all the strength he could muster. The stubby point of the brass poker punched in through Mister Tench's right eye, popping it like a small water filled balloon, and Parrish pushed on in a single movement, feeling the metal rod grate through the thin bone at the rear of the eye socket before jamming hard up against the inside of the back of the skull. Mister Tench never cried out. There was just a single, sharp intake of breath and a look of utter surprise in his remaining eye. His body seemed to lock up solid at the moment of death and Parrish held him there, poised on the end of his short spear before the body slowly tipped across him and fell almost in slow motion onto the fire.

For several long moments all Parrish could do was lay there, trying to recover his senses while at the same time watching in grim fascination as the dead man's clothing quickly changed colour, gave out a puff of smoke and smouldered for a second before fingers of flame began to lick at the body.

Only when Mister Tench did not move as the flames began to take hold did Parrish finally relinquish his hold on the poker handle and push himself away from the corpse. Elbowing his way backwards across the carpet he reached the nearest sofa and pulled himself up till he sat leaning back against it.

Ignoring the view before him he closed his eyes and tried to steady down his breathing and fight against the pain in his body. His ribs hurt when he inhaled too deeply and the small of his back ached with a pulsating throb that spread down into the base of his spine. He briefly put his hand there to massage the spot but it was very tender to the touch and he was a little surprised to find that his hand came away wet with blood. Strange, but for some reason the lacerations in his back didn't seem to be bothering him at all. Yet all these injuries were of a secondary concern. Bad as they felt, he knew they would heal quickly. As if waking from a sleep Parrish, no longer able to deny the call of his body, slowly opened his eyes and looked down at his left leg.

It felt as if it were on fire. Each pulse of his heart made the knee joint throb and the whole area felt gripped by an almost strangling tightness. He was acutely aware of the burning hot blood trying to force its way around the constricted veins and arteries there. The limb was already beginning to swell, the denim directly over the knee now smooth and still tightening. Lifting himself carefully onto the sofa Parrish sat slowly upright and gingerly attempted to set both feet on the floor. With no weight on it he was surprised to find that he still had perhaps thirty degrees of movement in his injured limb.

Using the firm leather arm as a support he tentatively lifted himself to his feet. This was a painful moment. His hands gripped tight the supporting arm and his head swam the moment he stood upright. He gasped as the blood rushed to his legs, every last drop of it seeming to wedge in his knee. But he gritted his teeth and the pounding subsided. Taking all his weight on his right leg and trying to ignore the pain in his ribs, he carefully set his left foot down and slowly applied some weigh to the battered limb. It just had to hold up. Needed to hold up, if only for a little while longer. There was still work to be done.

To his pain filled relief he found it would still suffer the strain of some of his weight, as long as he could bear the increase in pain, and it seemed he was still mobile too, if he kept the limb locked out straight. It was better that he had expected but less than he hoped. Still, on the positive side the tightness of the denim cloth around it would help keep it together, no matter how uncomfortable it felt.

With a grimace on his face and gritted teeth Parrish turned and hobbled across to the lounge door. Opening it carefully at first to be sure no one lay in wait on the other side, he moved out, not bothering to shut it behind him.

Not once had he looked back at the body in the mouth of the fire, the clothes on it now beginning to burn brightly. His attention was elsewhere, eyes urgently seeking out the entrance to the cellar.

20

Parrish hobbled in an ungainly, peg legged fashion down the passageway and reached the end door. Pushing it wide to reveal a huge kitchen, he leaned against the door frame and scanned the room.

Whoever had previously owned the house had clearly loved this room. It was immaculately turned out and fully furnished. Fitted cupboards ran around the walls, the floor was terra-cotta tile and there was an island worktable in the center of it. Hanging from ceiling hooks above this island were a great selection of pots and pans. A double sink nestled beneath the long window at one end of the room and a work top spanned the wall opposite Parrish, bracketed at one end by an old Aga and at the other by an ultra-modern gas cooker Attached to the wall above the work top was a long magnetic bar which held there a full display of kitchen blades. From small peeling knives, through long, thin fish filleting blades, boning and carving knives right up to and including a small selection of different sized cleavers, there was a knife for every job. A chef's dream kitchen.

But that was the last thought on Parrish's mind. He didn't think for one moment that Clouder cooked. Moving to the rack he pulled off a carving knife with an eight inch, serrated edge. He nodded in satisfaction. Sheffield's best and keen enough, long enough and nasty enough for the job ahead.

It was when he turned away from the display that he saw the cellar door he sought. Flush in the wall now opposite him, just to the right of the hallway door he had entered through, pine paneled with a thumb lift latch.

Strangely, he felt better now he was armed and beginning to close in. It was a stalk and as he moved across to the door he felt that adrenalin rush and the pain within him seemed somehow to diminish slightly as his concentration heightened.

Parrish slowly eased the door open, blade at the ready. There was a flight of steps leading down, ending at an apparently blank wall, the entrance to the cellar proper another door in the right hand wall at the bottom of the stairs. The faint drone of a muted voice could be heard floating up from below. Not switching on the light, he made his way down into the gloom, using the light from behind to see and the left wall as support. At the bottom he paused, squaring up to the closed door and listening to the louder but still indistinct words. A muffled, unintelligible noise that had a vaguely familiar cadence to it. Like a chant.

He pushed the door wide and stepped through, ready for anything, but pulled to a sharp, astounded stop at the sight before him.

All four walls of the windowless room were draped with some dark, heavy material that soaked up much of the already feeble light within the cellar. The light, coming from a single row of candles along the front edge of an altar table in the center of the room, cast flickering shadows against the few items in this darkened space. But this was not what stopped Parrish in his tracks. It was the big, hulking shape beyond the altar. There, close up to the back wall loomed a more than familiar, bulbous statue.

The Earth Goddess.

After the initial shock of her discovery, Parrish began to inspect the piece of work more objectively. Not as skillfully hewn as his own village's effigy and at about five feet high only a third the size, it was still unmistakably her. As he stared, eyes adjusting to the half-light, he began to see old pieces of stone of a different colour set into the statue. Old pieces fitted like jigsaw segments into the new stone, he realized. A part of his mind recalled the stolen piece of stonework from Danebury Museum and felt sure it was mated into this statue somewhere.

The curving lines of it shimmered in the almost pulsating candlelight, the effect remarkably close to that achieved by the holy ones. For a brief second he thought there was a holy man present too, stood between the altar table and the statue, his back to Parrish, arms raised as if in praise to her. But the man's carriage was all wrong and he knew without having to see his face that it was Professor Clouder. He wore a decorated bonnet and a cloak that wasn't festooned with wildflowers but had prints of flowers all over it. A pale copy of the real article but the essence of it was somehow right. Only at that moment did Parrish realize just how important it was that he complete the task Dannu and the holy one's had set him.

The moment he had entered the cellar cum shrine room the chant had stopped. A heavy silence fell as Clouder paused, in apparent deference to the Goddess or perhaps feeling the presence of a second person in the room, before slowly turning, a satisfied smile on his face.

“Thank you very much Mister Tench, I ..."

All expression dropped from his face, jaw slack and sentence unfinished as he stared, mortified, at the sight before him.

Parrish did not consider the fact that he might appear an apparition of horror before this man's altar table, although he knew he must look a sight. Blood still trickled from his gashed eyebrow, trailing down his cheek to drip onto his bare chest. The same eye was already beginning to close with the swelling. His chest was slowly discolouring with the onset of severe bruising and his bare torso was streaked with bloody smears from the wounds in his back. But Parrish read the shock on Clouder's face as the horror of realization that Mister Tench had ultimately failed and now he was totally unprotected.

“Mister Tench was good." There was quiet menace in Parrish's low, even voice. "Very good. You'll have trouble replacing him." He stepped slowly up, moving closer to the front edge of the altar table. "Except that you won't get the chance."

He had made himself more visible in the candlelight and Clouder now saw the gleam of the blade Parrish held down, apparently carelessly, by his side. The Professor was no fool. He had quickly learned that it was when this man appeared at ease that he was at his most dangerous. He knew too that he could not hope to match this warrior in combat, especially after he had bested his own champion, but there were other ways.

His next action surprised Parrish for instead of backing away, pleading for mercy or even leaping to the attack, he surprisingly calmly turned his back on the immediate threat to his life and once again raised his arms to the statue, calling out to her.

Parrish was shocked to hear the tongue of his people. The accent was stilted and the pronunciation of some phrases broken and jagged but it was unmistakably the language of those of Dannu's land, The voice of the ancient ones.

"Oh mighty Dannu," came the cry. "Woman of my power, bringer of the seasons and giver of life. I call upon those powers and energies of the long ages past to rise up and strike at the danger before me. I take now the light and the darkness. I summon up the anger of the stones and bring it into my hands. It is mine to control and I use it now to strike down my enemy."

As Clouder finished his chant he spun back to face Parrish, the light burning bright in his eyes. He lowered his outstretched arms until his hands pointed directly at the man before him.

"Die now, by the power taken by me from the Earth Goddess." he hissed and thrust his outstretched fingers like daggers at Parrish's face.

A sudden breath of wind passed through the room, making the candles between the men gutter. Then it was gone and they were once again just small flickering tongues of flame and light. Parrish simply thought the gesture rather melodramatic. Compared to his own holy man, this twentieth Century charlatan was pathetic.

With no trace of fear on his face, he coldly eyed Clouder in total defiance of the threat of death thrust upon him. He puffed out his chest, ignoring the pain in his ribs, and with his empty hand pointed one after the other to the marks on his body. As he did so he too spoke in the tongue of the ancients. It was as unexpected to Clouder as his own words had been to Parrish and the sound of it made the cloaked man's jaw sag once more and his arms drop limply by his sides.

"See me before you, false prophet. I am a warrior and these are my marks of honour. I am the bear killer. I am the wolf killer. I am the killer of my enemies and the killer of Chieftains. I am Parrish, Chieftain of Dane-bre. Leader of my people. Defender of their lives, their families and their village. I am known to the great holy ones who tend the temple of the Earth Goddess. You cannot threaten me, small man. She would not turn her own power against me." He pointed his finger directly at Clouder, the threat carrying in it immeasurably more power that the one uttered against him. There was a pause and silence reigned supreme for one timeless moment before Parrish uttered the final words. He did not raise his voice but the sounds seem to thunder around the altar room, almost striking against Clouder like a physical blow.

“This I know because I have been sent by her to stop you and your evil work.” And there was suddenly a great pride in his voice and a warm lightness in his heart as he understood the truth and announced it proudly.

"For I am Dannu's man!"

He raised the knife fully into view and advanced right up to the front edge of the altar table, his injured knee making him slow. It gave Clouder enough time to reach beneath the table. A handgun appeared in his fist and he leveled it at Parrish, who froze in his tracks. A nine millimeter Beretta. Current issue sidearm to most western armed forces, including Britain, and just about as deadly a handgun as you could get. Clouder grinned as Parrish eyed the weapon, knowing he had once again gained the upper hand. He flicked his wrist quickly, making the gun nod briefly to one side, and as if in complete understanding Parrish opened his fingers and the knife clattered to the floor at his feet.

The two men's eyes met.

"Yes." The insane glitter was bright in Clouder's eyes. "A gift from Mister Tench. In case all else fails he said. You're right, he was very good indeed and appears to have thought of every eventuality. D'you know Parrish, I really would love to have a long chat with you about your amazing knowledge of Dannu, but I'm afraid you are simply too dangerous." He shrugged. "So I guess I'll just have to kill you."

Parrish leaned forward, still much too far away from Clouder to even think about an attempt to grab for the gun. He rested his hands on the edge of the altar table, apparently to take some weight off his injuries, and spoke quietly.

"Go right ahead, if you have the *courage* to kill a man face to face and in cold blood."

The reply was just as quietly spoken and with just as much sarcasm. "Oh, but I have, I have."

And with that his finger tightened on the trigger, the double action mechanism within the pistol, pushing the hammer back towards full cock.

Parrish reversed his hands, gripped the edge of the table and with a great heave overturned it towards Clouder.

The pistol discharged, deafening within the confined space, as Clouder stumbled back and then fell against the base of the statue. The bullet passed very close beside Parrish's head but he was already moving back towards the door. Pushing his battered body to make good his escape put too much strain on his knee and it protested wildly. He cried out at the white hot flash of the pain.

Most of the candles had been extinguished as they hit the floor and in virtual darkness Clouder took the cry as proof of his shot striking home.

Scrambling to his feet as quickly as he could, he was just in time to see Parrish limp, in all too apparent agony, out of sight through the doorway. Ignoring all else, including the few still burning candles, one of which had come to rest against the bottom folds of the wall drapes, he kicked clear of the table and also went to the door, pistol out before him. The stairwell up to the kitchen was empty and he slowly, stealthily began to climb, not seeing the moment the smouldering cloth drape behind him ignited into flame.

Parrish, having gone up the stairs in a fast but untidy three pointed scramble, threw himself into the kitchen and sprawled there on the floor, gasping at the pain from his leg and ribs. But there was no time for rest. Not bothering to regain his feet he scrabbled quickly under the central table and pulled himself to his feet with the aid of the edge of the long work top opposite. On the wall right before him was the magnetic knife rack and he snatched the biggest cleaver from it then turned to face the cellar entrance. He could hear the slow, measured footsteps from below and knew he would be a sitting duck if he did not act and act now. Stifling all sound he hobbled back around the table and took up position beside the cellar door on the opposite side to the hallway entrance. He flattened himself against the wall and drew his arm back across his chest, the stainless steel blade high up by his left ear. Now it was a tense waiting game. But this was a game Parrish was a master of. He tried to calm his breathing and only then did he notice the faint smoke haze in the air and a certain odour that burned at his nostrils.

Clouder advanced slowly, taking his time as he moved up the stairs towards the light. The occasional blood smear on the walls bolstered his already growing confidence. He had seen that Parrish had taken a battering at the hands of Mister Tench and now, with a bullet wound to contend with too, he would surely be easy meat. He paused at the mouth of the stairwell. What he could see of the kitchen appeared to be deserted and he found himself inadvertently smiling. He was beginning to enjoy this and the prospect of tracking his wounded victim around the house before finally destroying him like an injured animal suddenly began to appeal. It was his first taste of the thrill of the hunt.

Parrish watched in total silence as the gun, arm, and then front edge of Clouder's body emerged beside him. And he saw the vital moment when, without any training to guide him, the man fell victim to his own natural instincts. For at that moment Clouder too noticed the faint smoke haze and then the smell. That awful smell! Burning flesh. It was a natural action of Clouder's body to turn, leading with his nose, and try to identify the source of the stench. As his head turned right towards the hallway door, Parrish, on his left, struck.

In a wide sweep the Danebury man brought the cleaver round in front of him and its keen edge went straight through Clouder's soft Adams apple and deep into his throat. The man's eyes went wide, the pistol dropped from his grasp, and a gargling noise came from his gaping mouth. With a sharp tug Parrish jerked his weapon free and Clouder sank to his knees, hands reaching for his throat as blood spurted and gushed in an incredible quantity from his neck. For a moment he just knelt there before the Chieftain of Danebury, hands trying desperately to stem the unstoppable flow, then he slowly tilted forward. Parrish helped him on his way, this time lashing down in an overhead chop, driven by all his remaining strength. The cutting edge went hard into the back of Clouder's neck just below the hairline, parting the neck as the blade cut through between the vertebrae. With a wet thud the body hit the tile floor and Parrish watched with a mixture of surprise and satisfaction as the head rolled on, skittering across the tiles before coming to rest against the cupboards opposite.

21

He wasn't sure quite how long he stood propped against the kitchen wall, just watching the blood flow from the neck stump and pool out around the corpse. It was as if his own body was somehow re-grouping, pulling itself together for one last effort. Only when smoke began to waft up out of the cellar stairwell did he come fully back to his senses.

That was it, he thought. That's the way to destroy all evidence of the Earth Goddess gathered by Professor Clouder.

He hobbled back to the lounge giving only a cursory glance at the burning body of Mister Tench before he started heaping as many pieces of combustible furniture that he could move on top of it. Even the pictures from the walls went on in an effort to stoke the flames and it was as he threw the smashed pieces of the coffee table onto the pile that a movement through the patio doors caught his eye. Something darting out there in the garden.

Slipping back against the wall he waited and a few moments later it was there again. He saw a man, sprinting between two clumps of shrubbery at the back of the garden, only just in his field of vision. A man clad in dark overalls, a beret and a black flak jacket. And he carried a weapon.

Parrish eased himself back into the hallway, a part of the building not visible from the outside thanks to that sturdy oak door. He had always known it would only be a matter of time but they had certainly moved quickly and he felt the hand of Litten at work. His shoulders started to sag as the inevitability of it struck home. He was all but finished.

In a way it was a relief. He hated the twentieth century. He had no life here and despised the lax and selfish attitudes of the people of these times.

Even the so called scientists who, in the name of research violated and desecrated the grave sites of those from the past, showed no honour or respect to those they disturbed. The thought of Klud's bones on display in a glass case stabbed at his heart. Yet Parrish did not want to be captured, although he knew that too was inevitable. In the eyes of these modern lawmen he had murdered. Knowing he had done no wrong and had in fact probably saved countless lives and untold mayhem and carnage would count for nothing in his defense. Even if he managed to escape this present situation he would be hunted down with no quarter given and without respite. Inevitably there was no escape. Everything would eventually come to light and the effect on his parents would be devastating, he suddenly realized, and surely they had already suffered enough?

So he came to a decision there in that quiet, lonely hallway. A decision as Chieftain of Danebury, not as a citizen of the twentieth century. There weren't many who chose their own time to die. And die he would but it would be as a warrior. Without shame or disgrace. With honour.

He took down his new combat jacket and gingerly tugged it on. Then he went into the kitchen. Going straight to the gas cooker he turned all the rings full on, the appliance letting out a satisfying hiss, then opened the doors of the double ovens and turned them on too. He figured both fires in the house were far enough away to allow the place to fill nicely with gas before igniting. Then he circled the table, first picking up the severed head by its hair then retrieving the Beretta. A quick check showed it to be fully loaded and the hammer cocked. He splashed un-noticing through the rapidly thickening blood pool and in a slow, resigned way limped back through the hall, into the lounge and right up to the patio doors, standing boldly before them.

Trophy in one fist, weapon in the other and face on to his enemies. This was how a warrior of the village of Dane-bre met death and went proudly into the arms of Dannu.

Outside in the grounds the men of the armed response units, under the direct command of Inspector Litten, were closing in. They were, even as Parrish was gathering himself up in the lounge, moving quickly and efficiently to their final positions prior to assaulting the building. Each man was tense. This was unlike any of their practice simulations for they had all heard the definite sound of a gunshot from within. This time it was for real.

One officer of the group moved past the single vehicle in the driveway and poised at the corner of the building. He looked back and noted with surprise the registration number of the BMW because he remembered it. It was the same one his old friend Chris had asked him to check up on. Coincidence? He pushed the thought to the back of his mind. There were more important matters to hand now. Moving stealthily but with speed, he darted towards the rear of the house. Peering warily around the corner of the building, he scanned his allotted section of the back garden and picked his spot, good cover behind a mature tree on the far side of the section of lawn before him. Taking a deep breath he pushed himself away from the brick work and sprinted across the short cut grass.

Almost as he reached the center of the lawn he saw in the corner of his eye movement in the patio doors directly to his left, his head instantly turning to look. A man had stepped into clear view, right behind the glass. An armed man. The police officer knew at that moment that his chosen tree cover, only fifteen meters further on, might as well be a thousand miles away. Caught in the open, he followed his training and skidded to a halt, dropping to one knee, his machine pistol coming to bear. But he did not fire. For the battered looking man in the combat jacket did not raise his own weapon and there was something about him. Something familiar. The officer felt as if he had seen him somewhere before.

"Police! Drop the gun!" he shouted. "And the ..." At that moment words failed him as he recognized with horror the object in the man's other hand.

Parrish had intended to simply walk out into the garden and be cut down but now watched in a bemused silence as a policeman suddenly sprinted out from nowhere and halted right in the middle of the lawn, not ten meters from where he stood. He saw the gun sweep up and then the man shouted but the words were indistinct through the double glazing. It didn't matter. All Parrish had to do now was raise his own gun in a threatening gesture and a bullet would come and take him. But before he could react a tingling sensation overtook him. Reflected in the glass just a foot in front of him was a sudden shimmer of blue light. Then every muscle in his body tensed and locked solid with a jerk, making him scream in agony as his knee and ribs screeched in protest.

The officer on the lawn saw the terrible pain on the man's face but that was only a secondary concern as he witnessed something else. Something shocking that he had seen once before, a long time ago. A faint blue glow suddenly surrounded the man behind the glass and the smoky air immediately around him seemed to thicken and twist. Then there was a bright, white, soundless flash and the policeman screwed his eyes shut against its sudden glare.

The resultant pressure wave exploded the plate glass panes outwards and a myriad of jagged shards lashed across the lawn, cutting through flowers and shrubs, embedding into the soft earth of the lawn and stabbing into the trunk of the tree off to one side.

But not a single piece touched the still kneeling officer.

Perhaps some unknown power was for that one crucial moment protecting him? Watching over someone who had once been a friend to Dannu's man?

The officer opened his eyes and stared, astounded at the sharp edged, glittering debris that surrounded him, before looking up to see that the man in the combat jacket had simply gone. Just like the time before, he recalled. But it couldn't be, could it?

Another policeman rushed up beside him and spun him by the shoulders, looking for injuries and dreading the worst.

“Are you all right, Bunny?" he asked, staring incredulously at the totally unmarked face.

Officer Rabbett nodded, dazed. He was sure of what he had just seen, but if he spoke of it to anyone, who would believe him? Then he knew just one man might. Chris Dunn.

“Well, c'mon!" The second officer pulled Rabbett roughly to his feet and together they stumbled back to the protection of the corner of the building. "You were fucking lucky then but Christ knows what could happen next."

As the last word left his lips there was a dull roar from somewhere inside the house, then a loud whoosh and every window in the building was pushed out by great tongues of flame as Mile End House erupted into a blazing inferno.

3,509 BC

22

The sound of the deafening thunderclap rolled away while the gathered clan of Dane-bre stared as one, agog at the empty space before the statue of the Earth Goddess. The empty space filled only a moment before by their Chieftain. The only people in the great shrine hut not to witness, yet still fully aware of his astounding disappearance, were the holy men gathered on either side of the shrine. They still chanted. With eyes closed and sweat beading on their brows, their concentration was absolute and unshaken, knowing their gargantuan task was not yet complete.

Then, as the thunderous rumble outside died away to silence, another just as recognizable sound made itself heard. Faint at first, but quickly increasing in volume. A cry. An agonizing, drawn out cry of pain. It somehow sounded far, far away then rushed in close with tremendous speed. In an instant the shout was right there inside the hut and again the air swirled in front of the statue of the Earth Goddess.

A bright light momentarily blinded the gaping onlookers and then the Chieftain of Dane-bre once was more stood before Dannu. To those gathered inside the hut the whole incredible event had taken no longer than the time it took to draw in a deep breath.

But they did not ponder on this amazing fact. Their ears were assaulted by his agonized cry and their eyes bewildered by his physical appearance. It was Parrish, but not the Parrish of a mere moment before. He now had no beard and his clothing had changed. But these were secondary considerations. He also now wore the unmistakable marks of battle and even carried a trophy!

On the instant Parrish reappeared the holy men released their great concentration, opening their eyes, ceasing their chant and sighing with the relief from the stress. A relief also felt by dozens of other holy men and many hundreds of other people in villages throughout the south lands. Each had played their part in the great coming together of hearts, minds and belief.

But only the holy ones at Dane-bre saw Parrish's physical state, heard his pain filled cry and felt his deep distress. As the exhausted man before them lapsed into unconsciousness, sagging forward and dropping what he carried, they rushed to catch him. They were not alone. Every person in the hut ran towards their Chieftain, eager arms outstretched to help him.

Parrish floated slowly up to consciousness, his body registering that he was laying flat on his back. After a brief flutter he opened his eyes. It took a few moments before proper focus was restored because one of his eyes was almost completely closed from bruising. A familiar sight finally emerged as he found himself looking up in confused amazement at the inner thatch of his own cabin.

His first reaction was one of disbelief and that he must be dreaming. Well it certainly appeared to be a dream. Something he'd wished to see but had accepted that he never would again. Then the damage to his body made itself felt and he drew in a sharp breath of real, honest to goodness pain. Turning his head to face where he knew his table and stools to be he saw a sight to gladden his heart. Juli, sitting in silence, patiently watching him. It brought an involuntary smile to his face. She smiled warmly back and came to his side, kneeling beside the bed, her hands resting lightly on the edge of the skins that covered him.

"I am back?" he asked softly, still not fully believing his eyes.

"Yes, my husband."

Three short words but the sound of her voice held untold reassurance. He wanted to laugh out loud. With a tender hand he reached out and touched her pretty face.

"It is like a dream. You do not know how much I have longed for this moment."

Juli clearly did not understand but smiled again while Parrish lay back and stared once again at the roof, trying to get to grips with the enormity of his experiences, what had transpired and just how it had all been accomplished. It was just unbelievable. The power the holy ones could control was astounding. And as for Dannu. Parrish recalled words he had heard only hours, or was it many centuries, ago.

"Her power came from the worship of her followers."'

If that was so the Goddess was truly capable of anything. She now commanded his utmost respect and deserved no less. Parrish now understood how, through his people, he was tightly bound to her and he suddenly hoped that what he had done in the future had been enough.

But all that was yet to come, millennia ahead. More important to him now was what had gone on here in his absence.

Propping himself slowly and painfully up onto one elbow he turned to face Juli. She had left him and was returning with a thick, padded roll of furs and put it behind him. He sank gratefully back onto the support, immediately more comfortable in the semi-reclined position. He nodded hisgratitude.

"Juli." He fixed her with a lop-sided gaze, the intensity of it freezing her in her tracks. He got straight to the point. Had to know. "Tell me. What has happened since I have been away?"

His wife frowned in puzzlement.

"I ... I do not understand. Nothing has happened."

"But I have been gone for many days. What has happened? What about the holy ones? The village that was outside? Danebre?"

The expression of bafflement on his wife's face deepened. After a long pause the look changed to one of disappointment. Disappointment that once again she could not answer her husband's questions because she was so stupid compared to him. All she could do was speak the truth.

"Nothing has happened, my Chieftain. What could happen?" It was Parrish's turn to frown as she tried to explain. "You have not been away. We saw you vanish before Dannu last night." There was a sudden look of wonder on her face. "It was a vision the whole village saw and we were all honoured to see the power of Dannu at work. But the vision was brief. You were gone, then in the blink of an eye you were once again back with us. As if you had never left. But we knew something had happened because of your strange clothing and your injuries." She shook her head. "I do not understand, my husband. You look as if you had fought a great battle, must have fought a battle, because you carried wounds and a trophy. But the head cannot have been won here in the land of the Earth Goddess, for surely we would have known and been with you?" She moved in closer and there was a pause before she could bring herself to ask the question she most wanted to know the answer to. Her voice dropped to a mere whisper. "Did ... did Dannu take you up to fight among the gods?"

Another time Parrish might have laughed at the funny side of her last remark. But after what he had been through there was no humour left in him. Perhaps Clouder might have seen himself as some tin pot god. Parrish just saw him as a menace.

Not answering Juli's question he relaxed back against the soft furs and motioned her to join him. This she did gladly and they lay together, holding each other, Juli silent while Parrish drew immense comfort from her nearness and tried to gather his thoughts. It was all too incredible for words, so he did not even try to form them. Who would he speak them to in this Neolithic age anyway? In the end he understood that he did not really care to explain it all.

He was simply glad to be back among his people and in their time. His proper time. A time that still had problems to be resolved.

He gave Juli a tender kiss then asked her to help him sit up. He wanted to know what the village was doing and was all at once concerned with the future prospects of his people and the agreement he had made with the Chieftain Shimon before the holy men of the temple of the Earth Goddess has whisked him away. As Juli pulled him up the pain from his ribs stabbed sharp in his chest. Finally upright he looked down at his covered legs, aware that his knee was not as painful as it should be, then gazed at his wife and asked two important questions.

"How far into the day is it, and how am I?"

A small smile escaped from Juli then. These questions she could answer, she just wished the news was better.

"The sun draws near to its height." she said evenly, knowing full well what it meant. Parrish just nodded as if it were simply an everyday observation. The tears welled in her eyes and a pleading look came to her face.

“You cannot fight today," she almost wailed. "Your injuries are too much!" As if to try and shock him into accepting the truth of her words she snatched away the bed skins to reveal his battered body. Parrish looked down at himself. No words needed to be said then.

He was well aware of his cracked ribs, his gashed and swollen face and the cuts in his back. Putting a hand there revealed the presence of a covering of poultice. A large wadding over more poultice was wrapped around his injured knee, clearly swollen out of all proportion to his right one. At least the magic mixture seemed to be keeping the pain down to a dull throb, although Parrish wasn't sure where that particular injury ended for much of the rest of his leg above the knee was discoloured through severe bruising. The length of the outside of his thigh in particular was a multitude of blues, browns, greens and yellows from the skillfully effective pounding he had received from Mister Tench.

"Yes, they are quite bad." he agreed. "But Juli, I gave my word. And as Chieftain it is my duty."

“But ... but ..." Her voice trailed away. He opened his arms and she fell into them, face buried in his chest. He ignored the pain and hugged her.

“Do not worry." he said softly. "I will do my best not to get killed today." It was difficult to keep the sound of confidence in his voice from slipping away. Juli just held him tight until he finally pushed her gently away from him.

"I need a crutch." His voice became firm and more businesslike. "You know, a long firm pole with padding at the top to tuck under the arm?"

“Like when my own legs were injured?"

"Yes." He smiled. "But long enough for me."

"Now?"

"Please."

She nodded and rose to her feet, wiping the tears from her cheeks. At that moment a call came from outside.

"Come!" shouted Parrish in return and a few moments later a hand held back the door blanket and the great holy one appeared, followed by his ever present aids.

Juli immediately cowered and bowed very deeply from the waist. The grey haired old man briefly and just barely acknowledged her, Parrish knew only because she was his wife, before moving to the foot of the bed. Juli looked pleadingly at her husband and he smiled and flicked his head to one side. She took the cue and darted out of the room.

The old man stood looking down at Parrish for a long moment before speaking. A smile came to his lips.

"Well, my young friend." That parchment dry voice. "You have certainly been at battle."

Parrish wondered just how much of what had gone one this old buzzard really knew. He nodded in agreement but was in no mood for small talk. There was one thing he needed to know himself.

"Yes. But was it enough? Have I done Dannu's bidding?"

The old man spread his arms wide and the smile expanded too.

"Parrish, the day is bright and clear. The sun shines and it is dry. Things are as they should be. She smiles."

The Chieftain of Dane-bre couldn't do the same. He was glad to have successfully completed his mission but helping out the Earth Goddess had dropped him in the mire. Soon he had to do battle with three good men and at the moment he wasn't even sure if he could stand up.

The holy one saw the concern on the face of Dannu's man and moved around to stand near at his side.

"Do not be too concerned." He said softly. "Things will unfold as they should now." There was a moment of genuine tenderness from him then as he leaned down and put a gnarled hand on Parrish's arm. "It was well done, my son. I know it was far from easy but you did not turn away. You have done Dannu, the people of the southlands, your people and yourself a truly great service. I speak for them all and for myself when I say thank you."

The personal acknowledgment meant more to Parrish than the other accolades and he smiled then.

"It was my honour." he said proudly.

The old man smiled warmly, patted his arm then straightened.

"Then I will leave you to your rest. You still have one more hard task ahead, great Chieftain of Dane-bre." He bowed deeply in respect, as did the attendant holy men. Parrish nodded back and as if it were a signal the three turned and left, without so much as a single rearward glance. Parrish watched in silence too.

“Still leaves me in the shit though." he said under his breath when they had gone, and lay back on his bed, thinking once more up into his roof thatch.

It was a while later when Juli returned with his rough and ready crutch. The shoulder end had been well padded with furs and after laying it alongside her husband to gauge the length she cut it to size. With her help Parrish gained his feet and after some painful moments of pounding blood he found he could stand with only minimal help from the crutch. He took a few tentative steps and, with gritted teeth, made a successful lap around the table before sitting back on the edge of the bed.

"It'll have to do." he hissed.

Juli couldn't hide the dread in her face. The dread of what was soon to come. Looking at the sunlight lancing steeply in through the open window port Parrish knew too.

“It must nearly be time." He said quietly.

As if his words were a cue another voice called from outside. This time a voice he recognized.

"Come!" he called gladly, struggling to his feet.

Klud pushed his way uncertainly through the door blanket, having never been in the Chieftains house before. He stopped in his tracks at the sight before him. Even though the tall man's body was terribly battered it was the look on his face that surprised him. Such joy.

“My friend!" cried Parrish, holding out his free hand. Klud went to him and they gripped each other’s forearm in the strange gesture the Chieftain seemed to like.

“You are all right, my Chieftain?" he asked.

"I am now." said Parrish gladly. "I thought that I might never see you again."

Klud frowned.

“But I have not gone anywhere?" he said. "And last night you were only gone for a moment. Why should we not see each other again?"

Parrish laughed. His friend’s basic logic was as firm as ever.

“You are right, of course. It was just that while I was away I saw things ..." Parrish’s voice tailed off as the image of bones under glass lodged in his mind.

“Visions?" Klud asked.

"If you like." Parrish saw the sudden keen interest in his friend’s eyes. “One day, perhaps, I might speak with you about them." Yet the moment he said it he knew he never would. "But not now. There is a task to be done. It is time, yes?"

The looks on both Klud and Juli's faces were answer enough. "Then I will be along in a few moments." He put his hand on Klud's shoulder. "I will need some help to get to the main gate but after that the task is mine and mine alone. Do you understand?"

"Yes, my Chieftain." the reply an unhappy growl.

"Then I will meet you outside shortly." He clapped Klud on the shoulder and the Neolithic man reluctantly turned and left the cabin.

Juli helped him dress then he sent her out first, taking a few moments alone to sort out what he would need. When he finally hobbled out into the sunshine he was confronted by the massed people of the village. The shock at his physical condition was clear on their faces but they all bowed respectfully.

In his new combat jacket and boots and a loose fitting pair of buckskins, all of which had been an effort to put on, he hoped he looked as commanding and intimidating as ever but still could not disguise his wounds.

Without a word of command from anyone he found himself lifted reverently onto a litter Klud had ordered made and he was carried rather ceremoniously down to the main gate. All the holy men had already gathered there. The oldest of the wise ones gave him a barely discernible nod. Then he was set carefully back on his own feet and handed his crutch. Klud and Tomps moved in close on either side and the village holy man stepped up behind.

“We will go with you as before." Tomps voiced the other men's thoughts. "And will stand aside as you have ordered. But say the word, my Chieftain, and we will gladly die in your place."

All the other warriors nodded in agreement and Parrish was

touched.

"Help me then to face them but whatever happens do not interfere or many will die on both sides." His tone was stern enough but there was warmth in his eyes.

Both warriors nodded and slowly, with Parrish trying his best to walk proudly, the three moved out of the hillfort towards those who waited beyond.

23

Chieftain Shimon waited patiently in the middle of the open land between the forest and the hillfort. At his back, some fifty meters or so away were those of his village, strung out in a line, expectantly ready to witness what was to come. Immediately behind him, shoulder to shoulder, were the same three warriors who had accompanied him during the previous day's confrontation.

All there silently watched in mild confusion at the slow and painful looking passage of Parrish and his group towards them. A confusion that changed to one of supreme confidence on the faces of Shimon and his three warriors as the poor condition of their opponent became clear.

Parrish, his own warriors and his holy man finally drew near and stopped about ten paces away. He opened his mouth to speak but checked any words, aware of a shuffling noise behind him. A glance over his shoulder left him somewhat shocked to find that all the people of his own village had silently followed him out and they too now stood some fifty meters back from their Chieftain. He was quite gratified and warmed by their show of faith in him. The only thing missing was their normally unshakable confidence in him. Their thoughts were clear on their faces. He couldn't blame them. As they saw it his present chances looked pretty slim. For a long moment the silence was total over Danebury.

Then Parrish ushered his escorting warriors to leave him. Klud stepped up close to take the man's crutch and as he did whispered under his breath.

"Just say the word, my Chieftain." he urged.

Parrish simply shook his head then sent him on his way with a tilt of his head. Then his attention turned to Shimon. He nodded at the man, who nodded cordially back.

“You do not look at your best, Parrish." He said bluntly. "Was it something to do with the wishes of the holy men? It seems they have kept you very busy."

In the twentieth century Parrish would have expected the remark to have been followed by a sarcastic laugh but Shimon's face and tone remained even. His was just a straight statement of observation. In the same vein Parrish did not expect a gentlemanly offer of postponement of battle till he was fitter either, nor did he get one. As he had earlier said to Juli, he had given his word and it was expected to be honoured.

"Do not concern yourself with my condition." he replied levelly. "Just remember our terms. When I defeat your men, you will answer to me."

It was then that Chieftain Shimon permitted himself a short laugh.

"*If* you defeat my men." he corrected. "But I remind you too of our terms. I have free run of your village and can take what I please from Dane-bre after you are dead." Once again the words came across as a plain statement with no attached sarcasm, although there was no attempt to hide the confidence there.

Parrish nodded again.

Shimon nodded and stepped aside.

As the three warriors now in plain sight moved about a meter apart and drew their war clubs, Shimon moved further away and stood a few paces off to one side, eagerness now showing in his eyes. The way the so called great Chieftain of Dane-bre looked now this fight was going to be no more than a formality. Then, as was agreed, he would clean the dead man’s village out of food, tools and even some of its women. And with little or no resistance. To him it was clear that the future of his battered village was now looking much brighter.

The warriors poised, eyeing the battered form of the Chieftain of Dane-bre. Each knew that alone they should easily be able to best this injured man but at that moment none was immediately willing to make the first move against the tall one rumoured to be close to Dannu.

The silence that fell back across the landscape only added to the hot tension cutting through the very air that surrounded everyone. Even the villagers of both camps founds themselves holding their breaths as the impending moment fast approached. The moment that would bring death to the field of battle before them.

Parrish's mouth set in a firm line. He knew what he had to do. Killing the three men before him was a price he must pay to prevent further killing. When they finally attacked him they would force his actions but he still found it so very difficult to justify to himself that he must sacrifice these few to save many. Each death would leave its mark upon his soul, a mark he would carry till the day he died, and he could not shake the knowledge that, however necessary, to him it was still murder.

Everyone watched in silence.

Shimon watched proudly as his men finally girded themselves up, yet at the same time was impressed with Parrish's apparently cool manner in the face of certain death.

The wisest of the wise ones watched coolly also, almost as if he already knew what the outcome would be.

Klud and Tomps watched hawk like, tensely coiled springs ready to leap on the instant to the defense of their friend.

Juli watched in dread. All the other villagers watched in tense expectancy.

Time.

Shimon's three warriors suddenly and simultaneously drew deep breaths, raised their weapons above their heads and lunged forward, charging in line abreast towards the Chieftain of Dane-bre.

At that same moment Parrish dipped his right hand into the pocket of his jacket, drew out Clouder's Beretta, pointed the deadly weapon and ruthlessly gunned down the three men.

The first two fell in quick succession with bullets through the heart. The third man, some unstoppable drive still pushing him on towards his fate, died instantly as Parrish took careful aim and shot him between the eyes when he was no more than ten feet away.

Every single Neolithic person there had flinched at the loud and totally unexpected explosions of sound from the hand of Parrish, rolling across the land like crashes of Dannu's thunder.

They witnessed too each man's fall and the full horror of it all gripped them as they saw the smoke bursting magically out from Parrish's outstretched fist and the back of the last man's head disintegrate in a mass of blood, bone and brains. The ground splashed red behind him as he was stopped in his tracks by some powerful yet invisible force, before crumpling limply to the ground. The body twitched once and was still. Horrific amazement froze every watchers face. There had been no physical contact at all and yet the three men were suddenly dead!

As if somehow connected, all heads then turned as one to look at Parrish.

Still motionless, the tall man's face was black as thunder and he swiveled slowly at the waist, bringing the mysterious black object in his hand around to bear on Shimon. The anger in his voice was treacle thick, only those who knew him well detecting the hint of self-loathing there. The Chieftain of Dane-bre looked on Shimon with fierce, blazing eyes and spoke slowly and clearly.

"You will do nothing further now! You will go back with your people to the edge of the forest and wait till I decide what to do with you."

Even though the eyes dared him to, Shimon still balked at being ordered around. He too was a Chieftain. He opened his mouth to speak but Parrish was having none of it and cut him short, thrusting the handgun even more threateningly towards the man. Shimon of course had no idea what the object Parrish held was, but he certainly knew what it did.

"Do anything else," Parrish hissed, real venom in his voice, "And I will turn the full power of Dannu on your village."

It was a blatant lie, he knew, but they did not know that and although the thought of what he had just done made him sick to his stomach, he dare not weaken now. Many lives could be saved now by boldness, or the three men laying at his feet had died for nothing. He raised his voice so as to be heard by everyone, eyes not once leaving the man now under his gun.

"Do anything else Shimon, and I will kill you and each and every single one of your people!"

A further ripple of shock ran through the gathered crowd. Even those of Dane-bre were staggered by the enormity of the threat. From behind Klud and Tomps came the quiet voice of the Danebury holy man. Quiet and clear as realization dawned.

“The wrath of Dannu is in him!" he gasped, and looked pleadingly at Shimon as he understood what could now happen. Three men had already died by the will of Dannu's man even while they had appeared to be still safely out of his reach. And although their deaths were a clear victory for the village of Dane- bre, the little shaman was shocked with the sudden prospect that the Earth Goddess was prepared to allow the imminent death of an entire village by the hand of her own man.

Chieftain Shimon saw the plain fear on the holy man’s face, at that moment truly believing Parrish’s threat. The colour drained from his face and he began to back slowly away from the tall man.

“As ... as you wish." He said quietly, now not caring about loss of face, only concerned with trying to keep the fear out of his voice and the people under his care alive.

"Then go."

Shimon found himself bowing to Parrish before turning and heading gladly away from the man, back towards his still shocked people.

Parrish held the pistol on the man's back for a moment longer then the breath sighed out of him and his gun hand dropped limply to his side. Klud and Tomps appeared at his elbow and he thumbed on the safety and pocketed the weapon before accepting their shoulders under each of his arms for support.

Without further regard for the villagers opposite the two warriors turned him around and helped him back toward his own people. As the three passed the still motionless holy man Parrish said quietly.

"Let them collect their dead and offer them up to the sky spirits on our mound. They do not have one of their own."

The little shaman nodded. He knew by now not to ask if the Chieftain wanted any trophies.

The litter was produced from among the Danebury crowd and he was laid gently on it and carried back to the hillfort, the holy ones leading the way.

Parrish just lay back, eyes closed, his self-disgust not letting him look anyone in the eye. The gesture went un-noticed. Some of his people at that moment did not want to stand quite as close to their Chieftain as they usually would.

They had never before seen something that frightened them so much.

24

Before facing Chieftain Shimon again Parrish allowed himself a full week in restful recuperation before attempting to take to his feet once more. Although in fact no one but he knew a week as a time span, the period seemed right for him to make his plans, rest his battered body and allow the excitement at his so called victory to ease somewhat.

But he was by no means idle during that time. Several ideas were set in motion and a number of visitors received.

For the most part though Parrish could be found outside his cabin, propped up against the south facing wall on a well padded bed, sometimes laying back with his young son either in his arms or close by his side while they both slept. The people of the village puzzled only briefly over this. Normally a warrior had little or nothing to do with newborn sons until they became old enough to begin learning the ways and skills of men. But then, the Chieftain of Dane-bre was no normal man. Even if he wasn't physically present among the villagers he could always be seen outside his house, simply watching over his village and soaking up the warming and much welcomed sunshine. He was blissfully unaware that it was sunshine his people believed shone down because of his mysterious efforts while in the spectral realm of the Earth Goddess.

The tall man's knee was swathed in regularly changed wrappings that held in place fresh helpings of that heady smelling, healing poultice. Always applied by Juli, although he knew she had no need to actually make the stuff. Many other wives were more than willing to do this task and in doing so had the blessings of their men folk. The warriors saw it as their way of helping in some small way, for any assistance that would aid their leaders healing they were more than glad to offer.

All Parrish's cuts had scabbed over without any sign of infection, his ribs had been securely strapped and his bruises had blossomed into multi-colored hues. Juli spent virtually all her time fussing over her man and Parrish was ashamed to say that he let her carry on unnecessarily sometimes, thoroughly enjoying her applications of tender love and affection. The soft smile on his face and apparent total lack of concern for his own injuries made her frown all the more as she plumped up his padding and offered him the umpteenth bowl of that reviving if not particularly nice tasting broth.

"Only ugly for a while." he told her with a lopsided grin. Juli saw nothing at all funny in the remark.

One of the first things Parrish did, the very next day after his killing of Shimon's men, was to suspend Dane-bre's next, already arranged, hunting trip. He made it clear that he wanted his people to stay within the boundary of the hillfort for a while, only those tending to the flocks, maintaining the field systems or going to fetch water allowed to leave the safety of the walls. This of course meant mostly women only who had permission to leave the village. He felt the ripple of unease flow through the village at this order, particularly among his warriors, but no one questioned it. They knew there was always a reason for his actions and commands, no matter how odd some of those reasons might be.

Using the Danebury holy man as a willing and impartial mediator, he informed Chieftain Shimon that to help the man's people until his decision was made, the Chieftain of Dane-bre would allow Shimon's warriors to go out on a hunting trip to feed their people. There would be no resistance or interference from the village of Dane-bre, leaving the party to hunt unhindered and bring in fresh meat to the sprawling encampment of wicki-ups that had sprung up along the forests edge. They were rather a sorry looking sight, reminding Parrish of a hastily erected refugee camp. This encampment was now being referred to by the people of Dane-bre as the village with no roots.

Word had come quickly back from this place that Chieftain Shimon was grateful and, from his high vantage point Parrish watched in silence as an armed party set off into the forests not long after the high of sun the same day. They must already be quite low on provisions, he realized, and judging by the size of the hunting party there could not be a very large contingent of warriors left behind to guard the women and children. It once again impressed Parrish just how much faith was put on a man's word here. He had said no interference and Shimon and those of his village believed him to the point of leaving themselves somewhat exposed, to the point of almost putting their livelihoods and lives on the line. All on the strength of one man's, *his,* word.

While the hunting party was gone Parrish called Klud and Gant to his bedside.

The two men arrived full of curiosity. They hoped to find some insight into what the Chieftain intended to do with the village without roots, after all there might be an opportunity for trophies, but there might also be a chance to get a glimpse at that mysterious, all powerful, black death giver from Dannu that he had not so long ago commanded with great effect. They were to be disappointed on both counts. Parrish simply sent them on a survey.

“My friends and brave warriors.” he said as the two arrived. At once they sat down beside him, not wanting to insult the great man by standing over him. Neither did they comment on the strange look of his still bare chin. "I have called upon you to do a task for me."

“It is our honour." they said almost as one.

Parrish smiled. The pair were perfect for what he had in mind. He wanted Klud to go simply because he valued the man's open and forthright opinions, the only man of Dane-bre not in total awe of his Chieftain and ready to say exactly what he thought. Gant on the other hand might not be so forthcoming, but he was a born planner and organizer. He could quickly see building works in his mind’s eye and gauge manpower and materials. This was the skill Parrish really needed most at the moment.

“I want you both to cross the east river.” He pointed out beyond the burial, knoll. A few kilometers beyond it, hidden from sight in the valley was the water course known simply to his people as the east river. Parrish knew it as the river Test. "Go to the next hill beyond it." The two men followed Parrish’s gaze to the prominent hump on the skyline in the middle distance. “Explore it. See what is beyond and around it. I want to know if it would be a good spot for a camp."

Klud nodded at that. He grinned in understanding

"Yes. You intend to move Shimon's people further away so we can plan an attack without being watched."

Parrish started to shake his head but quickly turned it into a knowing nod. Klud was a true warrior but sometimes his thirst for blood was almost too much. Yet this time it could be worked to good benefit.

“Good thinking, Klud. When you are there see how it might be possible to attack the hill. Where are the best approaches and so on." There was a second nod from the Neolithic man.

He then turned directly to Gant. "My friend. I want you to look fully at the ways and means of the hill as an open site and think about how it might be a good place for the building of a camp."

His words could almost have been taken as an insult, for Gant he knew would never give any task less than one hundred percent, would never consider doing only half a job. But the man simply nodded at his leader and said gravely.

“I will give it my full attention, my Chieftain."

“Then I could ask no more." He smiled broadly at them both. "Thank you my warriors. Come and see me as soon as you return."

It was the Chieftains way of saying that the meeting was over and without further ado they both bowed while still seated, then rose to their feet and set off back down the hill, soon deep in discussion with each other.

It was somewhat of a surprise to Parrish when his warriors did not re- appear until late the following day. From the observation post that was his sick bed he had misjudged the distance between Danebury and the hill across the river.

Had the services of a modern aerial surveyor been available to him he would have been told that the straight line distance, as the crow flies, between the two sites was six and a half kilometers. Across the ground, that made it at least eight and with a river crossing to boot. After he had fully recuperated Parrish would eventually walk the distance himself and gain this knowledge.

Thus, considering the average speed at which Neolithic people moved across the countryside, the distance easily amounted to a half days travel. Klud and Gant, as good as their word and spending many hours examining the hill and its surrounds, decided against travelling at night especially with an enemy so nearby. They bedded down among the yew trees there, returning to their village and Chieftain the next morning.

The two duly delivered their reports and Parrish thanked them for their dedication and efforts, sitting in silence for a long time afterwards mulling over the information received.

The following morning, the sixth day of his self-enforced bed rest, he had another, most important visitor.

Alone, slowly moving yet steadily climbing the slope to the Chieftain's cabin, came the wisest of the wise ones. Parrish, resting with eyes closed did not witness the laboured approach, only blinking awake at the sound of a polite cough close at hand.

"Oh!" was all he could say in surprise and made to rise to his feet. The grey haired old man pushed him gently back down with a gnarled hand.

"No need to rise Parrish, I will sit. Indeed, I am in need of the rest." He smiled his charming, innocent looking smile, the one that always brought Parrish to full alert.

With a soft sigh the old one lowered himself carefully to the ground and settled back against the wall of the cabin beside Parrish.

"Ah." he said after a long moment of silence. "I see it now. And so do you. The people below speak of your eyes upon them from up here."

"Oh." said Parrish again, this time in dismay. "I did not know they were upset by me looking down ... "

"No, no." came the quick interruption. "You misunderstand. They know they are not being looked down on. They know they are being looked *after*."

"I ... see." said Parrish, not at that moment quite sure if he did.

"But that is not why I have come to speak with you, my young friend. I believe you have some plan for Shimon and his people. If you feel you can, I would be glad to hear what, if any, of this plan you can tell to me."

"My apologies." said Parrish. "I would be happy to tell you, and be glad of your thoughts on it. But I expected you to be here to see it for yourself."

"Ah, but if only I could. Yet I and my own people must return to the great temple. There is much to do there with the high of summer fast approaching.

Like you, I too have responsibilities to others. Besides, our part in the tasks done here at Dane-bre has been completed. But I would like to know what is to become of Shimon and all that remains of his village. That knowledge might be helpful to the holy men at the next gathering."

Parrish nodded in understanding then. The old man was still as canny as ever.

So the Chieftain of Danebury told the grey haired wise one of his ideas and proposals and what he hoped they might achieve. The holy man listened in thoughtful silence with only the occasional nod as comment.

Finally, Parrish too fell silent, looking to his companion for approval or rejection. He knew whatever the old man said would be the deciding factor, for if he turned the proposal down it would be as good as dead. Parrish would never ask his people to go against the living symbol of their religion. He was well aware of their total dedication to their Goddess and her servants. He wasn't aware though that his people realized some important moment was being reached up above them in the shelter of the house of their Chieftain. They knew not what the two men spoke of but all were watching with curiosity and a deep respect, the pow-wow in progress between Dannu's man and her high priest. It was a time that would be talked of around campfires for a long time to come.

For a long while the old man stared down at Dane-bre, occasionally glancing away to the hill in the distance, across to the collection of wicki-ups at the forests edge and back again. Then he turned to face Parrish.

“It is most unusual. Never been tried before.” He paused. “But I do see your reasoning’s and there are great possibilities there." He patted Parrish on the shoulder and smiled that smile. “It is bold and worthy of a chance. If Shimon, his people and yours can be won over, I give you my blessings on it."

Parrish grinned widely. He knew he could not have asked for more, but felt he must, even though he had no right to.

“If the plan is not too well received,” he said slowly, “can I tell them all that you have given it much thought and agree with it?”

The old man did not even pause before replying, as if somehow knowing that things would unfold as they should.

“If needs be, yes."

“Thank you.” Parrish bowed as best he could in his reclined position.

Without acknowledging the heartfelt thanks, the old man struggled gainfully to his feet, making good use of the sturdy wall at his back, then took a pace back and looked down on the tall man he liked so very much.

"You are a wise man, Parrish. Your thoughts and deeds do you great credit. I am proud to know you and Dane-bre is most fortunate to have you. Be well, my son, and I will see you again when you bring your people to the great gathering." There was a coy pause before he added. "You will make time to visit an old man when you are there?"

"It would be my honour." replied Parrish gravely before breaking into a broad grin.

The wise one smiled back then and, with a final bow of respect to the Chieftain of Danebury he turned and headed back down towards the great shrine hut, leaving Parrish with the grin lingering on his face and a warm glow in his heart.

25

An air of grudging acceptability had settled over the land around Danebury as the days passed without any direct confrontations between the two camps. A weather eye was of course kept on each village by the other but the tension eased off as the day to day running of life took over from the 'standby for battle' attitude that had initially held the upper hand. It was the beginnings of acceptance of the proximity of others, and what Parrish had been waiting for.

The time was as right as it would ever be.

Now back on his feet but still very dependent on his crutch, the pain easing poultice and suffering a severe limp, Parrish got to work.

Once again using his holy man as a go between he requested that Shimon grant him an audience at the high of the sun in the great shrine hut. As a gesture of good faith he could bring some of his own warriors with him. For protection if he liked, although Parrish would rather they were considered a more ceremonial escort. He next gave instructions to Klud concerning his own men, then could do no more than wait for the allotted time.

Once all these things were set in motion he limped back into his cabin to spend some time with his family and no doubt ponder over the possible options and probable outcome of the imminent meeting. Not only was the man's health gradually returning but his natural stealth was returning too because, unaware that he was making very little noise, he entered the cabin, pulled back the door blanket and found Juli, unaware of his presence, seated motionless at the table. Her concentration was total on the object before her where her husband had casually placed it several days earlier. Black and inert, the handgun looked totally unnatural and out of place against the background of natural timber and earth around it. The Neolithic woman would not dare touch the object but she almost bristled with curiosity over it. She placed a hand tentatively above it as if expecting it to be hot, then sniffed at it, nose wrinkling up against the oil laden vapour it gave off. At that moment Parrish reached over her and plucked the weapon up from the table.

"Oh!" she gasped. "I am sorry ... I just ..."

Parrish simply smiled and kissed her on the cheek. He had not fully realized the height of curiosity the gun would cause.

“Do not worry." he said softly. "If you really want to look at it you had but to ask."

"But it is from Dannu!" She blurted. "And for you alone to use. I thought that if I asked, you would become angry."

From Dannu? Parrish considered the revealing words for a moment before answering. This piece of twentieth century technology could cause more trouble than he had realized.

“Do all the people believe it is a gift from the Earth Goddess?" he asked almost too casually.

Juli nodded emphatically. As if he didn't already know, she thought.

"I see."

Parrish stared down at the handgun in his open palm, deep in thought. It dismayed him to think his people considered this murderous piece of hardware a gift from the Gods. He decided to let Juli see it once more. Really see it for what it was, just a collection of metal components, before putting it well out of sight of everyone.

Sitting down opposite his wife he deftly popped the magazine and ejected the remaining eleven rounds from it with his thumb. After gathering them into a little pile to one side he slapped the magazine back home into the base of the grip, pulled back the slide to check the chamber was clear then let it slide forward into battery with a loud metallic ‘clack’. All the while his wife watched, open mouthed in total fascination. Finally, he dry fired the weapon, squeezing the trigger to make the hammer snap down. Grasping the pistol by the muzzle he offered it across the table to Juli.

"I have made it safe now." he said. "Feel it, point it and play with it if you like."

She took it as offered, still afraid of the object not from this earth but having no intention of refusing her husband and offending him. At first she just stared at it in her tiny fist, trying to decide if it felt hot or cold. The texture of the ABS plastic grips defeated her senses. It seemed to be neither. Nor did it hurt or burn the hand of a mere mortal and her confidence quickly grew. At arm's length it was heavier than she had imagined but was not too difficult to point.

First twisting her wrist to see how it looked from both sides, she then experimentally swept the room with it. Parrish instinctively swayed away as the muzzle of the pistol swept over him.

"It makes no noise now." she said in a puzzled tone. And a good job too, thought Parrish.

"No. Because it is not for this time." he replied, knowing she would not understand. "You are the only one to have touched this ... gift from Dannu ... but do not feel honoured. It is a bad thing. It is a killer of warriors before they can even defend themselves. It has no honour and gives those who would use it no honour."

She frowned and Parrish was glad she did not understand. He smiled across at her and got up, went to his Army webbing and returned with his issue, green, hinge-lidded tobacco tin that contained his rifle cleaning kit. Under Juli's wide eyed, all seeing gaze he deftly stripped the pistol down into its component parts, cleaned and oiled them all then re assembled the weapon He asked her for a large square of soft leather which she quickly produced from among the pile of assorted pieces kept for repairs or small items. Parrish carefully wrapped the pistol up in it along with its ammunition and secured the bundle with some cord. He rose again and limped across to the chunky stone fireplace and, reaching high up placed it on a stone ledge there, well out of reach of all but he. Turning to face Juli he said coldly.

"Only you and I know where it is. It is never to be taken down from there unless I especially ask for or order it. OK?"

Juli nodded, a mixture of confusion and fear flashing across her face.

Parrish hobbled back across the room to her, smiled and bent at the waist to kiss her.

"Now, enough of this. Come, I have a very important meeting to attend and it would make me feel better to have you at my side."

Juli nodded, honoured that her husband felt the need of her. It was true enough but Parrish had an ulterior motive for the request. He knew that whatever she saw and heard at the meeting would soon be passed on to all the other women of the village. And thus, onto the women of Shimon's village too. It was his way of making sure that *everybody* knew what was going on and what was expected of them. It was a wise Chieftain who made use of all channels of communication open to him!

At the high of the sun Chieftain Shimon along with his holy man and four of his warriors, good men judging by their tattoo's, entered the gate of Dane-bre. The small band moved through the village towards the great shrine hut under the astounded gaze of the women folk and acutely aware of the complete absence of any warriors. Strange warriors entering a village, while still alive let alone under their own steam, was an unheard of event, never mind going on to enter another Chieftains shrine hut! They had expected a heavy armed presence but found nothing. Moving in total silence through the buildings of the village they made their way straight to the shrine hut. At the entrance they were met by the Danebury shaman who ushered them inside. Shimon led through the door blanket and along the partition passageway before the little group emerged into the hut proper, stopping dead in their tracks at the sight before them.

At the mouth of each of the stalls that ringed the interior of the building stood the man who's stall it was. All of Dane-bre's warriors were there, a great circle of men with their Chieftain at their head, standing tall in the mouth of his own stall, directly across from the entrance and beside the statue of Dannu.

Shimon's first thought was that he had been lured here to be killed but before he could act the tall man held out his hands.

"Chieftain Shimon." he said loudly and warmly. "Welcome to my village and to the house of Dannu."

At that every single warrior in the great circle bowed deeply from the waist as a sign of respect. The action almost unnerved Shimon and it was a few moments before he could pull himself together and force his legs to move. With slow, deliberate strides he crossed the hut, walking around the central fire and coming to a halt before the tall man. His own warriors flanked him but none had even attempted to draw their weapons. They knew as well as their Chieftain that to attempt battle against so many would just bring a swift death.

Shimon stood before Parrish, boldly holding eye contact, noticing only peripherally that the Dane-bre holy man had taken station on the man's left. The warrior known as Klud stood at his right and back in the stall behind him was the Chieftains wife.

Rather unexpectedly, Parrish did not immediately address Shimon, but the second holy man standing behind him. Parrish thought he recognized the face but could not place it.

“And what is your part in this?" he asked, his tone one of simple curiosity, no aggression there.

“The village of Shimon is without a holy one." The shaman put on a brave face and spoke loudly but his voice almost cracked on that first word. The wise one had told him to expect bold and different actions from the tall man but he still found this first direct contact with him somewhat unnerving. He also found himself explaining when he didn't need to. "Their man was lost to Dannu when the village was destroyed. The wise one has given me the honour of staying to take on his task for Chieftain Shimon's people."

Parrish just nodded in understanding. Only then did he turn directly to Shimon.

“Would you join me in my stall? We can now talk of what I have decided should be done."

The reply was a curt nod and the pair moved in and sat down on the soft straw, Parrish taking his time, being careful not to jar his injured leg. Shimon's men took up station in pairs on either side of the stall entrance, looking with steely eyes out into the hut, but it was a gesture of protection only. The two Chieftains sitting down was a clear signal for every other warrior to also sit, no one wishing to offend either leader by standing over him. Parrish smiled.

“That is better. Now, to business."

In the silence that followed the sentence he could almost hear every ear in the place flapping.

26

It was at that moment that Chieftain Shimon could bear it no more. No more uncertainty. No more being led by the nose. No more being kept in the dark while the life or death of what remained of his village hung in the balance. As Parrish opened his mouth to speak once more he jumped in first, normally an unforgivable interruption.

"The only thing I need to know is are my people to die!" The sentence exploded from his lungs, desperation hot in his voice. Desperate to know the answer and desperate to try and regain some sort of control over his destiny. "I tell you now, we will not give up without a fight!"

The hush inside the great hut was total then, the open threat hanging in the air.

Parrish's face remained expressionless but inside he rejoiced. The Chieftain had finally shown his true colours. This was a man of strength and conviction. A good Chieftain, who was fully committed to his village and the people under his care. Parrish now knew he could deal with this man on level terms and understand where his loyalties and intentions lay.

"That will not be necessary." He replied slowly and watched the relief flood into Shimon's face. "But there are still problems to be sorted out. I have given your position much thought." He paused. "If you and your people are willing to work together with me and my people, I have a plan that can solve those problems."

"Work together?" Chieftain Shimon's chest puffed out and his voice became stern. "My people do not need outside help. We have the will to survive. With skill, courage and the blessing of the Earth Goddess, we will carry on."

Parrish smiled at him, disarming his aggression. "I would expect no less from a good village led by a great Chieftain. What I have in mind is more of an agreement rather than physical help. An understanding."

There was another silence. Parrish watched intently as this first, vital hurdle was approached. He knew Shimon was simply considering his people's position, being as they were undermanned and unprotected against the stronger, determined village of Dane-bre. And as Parrish had correctly surmised, the man himself was not stupid. He found himself holding his breath as Shimon braced up for his reply.

"I can promise nothing but that I am always ready to listen." he said slowly.

"Good man." said Parrish quietly in English, the foreign words bringing looks of puzzlement from those around him. He quickly reverted to the language of his people. "Very well. This is what I propose." He knew he already had the undivided attention of one and all but was surprised to find, as he glanced briefly out of his stall, that every warrior in the place was now gathered and seated at the entrance to it. He had not heard them close in. What struck him as most significant about the sight was that among this group of warriors sat Shimon's own men, shoulder to shoulder and indistinguishable from all the rest. A symbol perhaps of the future, he thought. His gaze returned to their Chieftain.

"You and your people are low in strength and without a village. I cannot replace your lost warriors but I can offer you a new home, in return from a few agreements from you and your people."

"Agreements?" Shimon did not enjoy the experience of having his people's precarious position stated openly, but still found himself filled with curiosity as well as suspicion.

"Listen." Parrish dropped the Chieftain to Chieftain formality and leaned in, trying to talk to Shimon as a friend. "I have already started to check on my ideas and this is what I offer you.

Just over half a day's walk from here, on the far side of the east river, is a hill suitable for the siting of a village. My men have visited it and told me of what they saw." At that Klud nodded. "There is good land beyond it and it offers a good position for huts and defensive ditches. With hard work and determination you and your people could settle there." Several men rocked back at that. Klud frowned deeply but said nothing, knowing his Chieftain well enough to hear him out fully before making any judgment. Shimon said what everyone was thinking though.

"It is too close to Dane-bre. There would be fighting."

Parrish nodded.

"There would be, yes. And that is why there is need of an agreement." He plunged straight on, there was no turning back now. "Half a day's travel is far enough apart for our peoples not to bump into each other during normal day to day work. But there will be hunting parties and other odd occasions when our peoples might meet. What I want is your word of honour, on behalf of all your people as well as yourself, that if they should meet then each would simply accept the presence of the other and just walk away. A joint agreement to deny a battle. An agreement *not* to fight without the sole word from their Chieftain. Both you and I only would hold responsibility and so there would be no loss of face for our warriors."

Shimon's surprise at this suggested course of action was plain enough on his face. It was plain on everyone's face.

Parrish could almost hear all their Neolithic minds working. This was something unheard of. He was asking warriors to pass up on chances for trophies and glory, not just from his village, but from another one too. For the men of Dane-bre this would be twice as hard for they had superiority in both strength and numbers. He let everyone chew on their thoughts for a few seconds more before continuing.

"The chances of fighting could be further cut if we could both agree on a line between our two villages. Not to be crossed unless permission is given by a Chieftain. My idea for this is the east river between the two village sites. I suggest your people stay east of the water way and mine this side. If both camps abide by its boundary the chances of clashes would be even less. Enough I think to enable both villages not to live in constant fear of attacks from the other."

Shimon thought carefully for several tense moments before nodding slowly. The logic of the statement clear even to him.

"That would be true." he said slowly.

Parrish caught the faint smell of success and pressed home the advantage.

"Yes. If you stay on one side and we on the other it would work. There is still plenty of usable land to the east and the hunting parties who go north might meet but then only by chance. If they could be ordered to just walk away from each other war between the two villages could be avoided."

"It would be difficult." Shimon's words again came out slowly but that was because of the thought which was behind them. "But not impossible."

He was indeed milling over the tall man's proposal but putting it against his own agenda. The welfare of his people was paramount and he had been pondering for several days on how to keep them alive and the chances of re-establishing those left under his charge into a village of some kind. Such closeness to another village had not even entered his mind but the Chieftain of Dane-bre's suggestion, strange as it was, suddenly seemed to be the best of any options he could think of. He could of course refuse and take his people on to try and find some other place, but the longer he delayed the smaller and weaker they became. And that made them easy prey. He tried to look for some hidden scheme behind the strange yet at the same time sensible offer.

"And if I and my people agree to this arrangement, what would be your benefit from it?"

Parrish could smell success more strongly now.

"There are some benefits for my village which will only become clear after a time. But let us just say for now that I would be glad simply to have helped another village on Dannu's land. I believe she does not frown on this idea and I for one would not wish to go against the will of the Earth Goddess."

There were gasps from some warriors. This plain implication that Parrish had talked of his plan with the Earth Goddess herself only reinforced their belief in him as Dannu's man. It also implied that if Shimon refused Parrish's suggestion he would be running the risk of perhaps denying her. Parrish ignored the sharp intakes and spoke directly at Shimon, a sudden harshness in his voice.

"Do not think I am being soft on this matter, my friend, simply to be kind to the Earth Goddess. The safety of my village always comes first and if you or any of your warriors breach our agreement and heads are taken, I would gather up my men and *all* the powers I can muster." There was a pause that seemed to emphasize the enormity of the threat. "With them I would come for you and wipe your new village from the face of Dannu's land. Know now Shimon that once you have given your word I will hold you to it fully. Break your word of honour and you would feel my fury. Not a single man, woman or child of your village would live to see another morning sun. No stick or stone of your village would be left standing high enough to cast a shadow."

Parrish knew his threat had to be bold and plain enough but his inner thoughts could not have been further from his words. His greatest hope was that the agreement would hold for a long, long time. Long enough for friendships to grow between the peoples of both villages. Long enough that there would be exchanges of ideas, bartering of goods and eventually even inter village marriages. The two villages could perhaps one day accompany each other on the long walk, offering strength and solidarity against the other villages of the south lands. The chance of achieving such things would be worth taking a risk for. But all this would only come about if Shimon could convince his people, as Parrish must convince those of Dane-bre. This boundary of the east river, the river Test, would hopefully keep both factions apart long enough for them to get a little more used to their nearness to each other.

Shimon believed completely the weight of Parrish's threat but it did not concern him unduly. Once he had given his word he would never dream of he or any of his people breaking it. His thoughts were more focused on the possible and far reaching implications of this monumental proposal. But he knew as well as Parrish that he had the weak hand. He had nothing to bargain with, his only other option was to take his people away. And yet the chance to be near enough to a village for regular bartering for goods, grain and equipment, something his people had little or none of, would clearly be of great benefit. It would make re establishing a new village and preparing it for the next winter so much easier. Give his people more of a chance. A chance to live.

The longer Shimon took chewing over the proposal the more Parrish was sure he had won. But he dared not count his chickens yet, even if there had been any such fowl about in 3,500BC.

Chieftain Shimon stared at Parrish for a long time before inhaling deeply, his decision made. But he did not want it to seem, before all these men, that he had too easily bowed down to the man before him.

“I must of course talk of this with my people. Their lives are in my hands but what you ask must be understood fully by them all."

“I understand. It is the same for me but there are great possibilities here, for both our villages, if the people can see it and it is the will of Dannu.”

“Yes." Shimon could not deny that. He rose to his feet and in an unexpected gesture offered his hand out to Parrish, who gratefully accepted it and pulled himself gingerly to his feet.

“I will give you my answer in the morning.” Shimon bowed to the tall man, signaling that the meeting was at an end. Parrish smiled broadly and bowed in return.

“And I will come to your hut to receive it.” he said warmly, surprising everyone. "You have visited me here and so I would like to return the honour."

“The honour is mine.” Shimon bowed one more time, turned and, with head held high, stepped out of the stall. All the warriors there, now on their feet, parted to allow him passage. His own men fell quickly and quietly in behind him. Parrish turned to Klud and said quietly.

“Escort our guests to the gate.”

Klud nodded again and went after the departing group. Parrish waited till they had gone from sight before allowing himself a broad smile of satisfaction and sinking slowly back down onto the soft straw. As if reading his mind Juli appeared at his side with a clay beaker of water. Totally ignoring the stares of his gathered men he took a long, deep draught of the cool liquid then grinned at his tiny wife.

“That went rather well, don't you think?"

Like the still silent holy man and all the warriors before her, Juli could only stare on in utter amazement.

Shimon and his four warriors walked in silence through the

village of Dane-bre towards the main gate, Klud at their head as a one man guard of honour. Several women swung the entrance wide as they approached and the group stepped out, giving them an uninterrupted view of the Neolithic landscape. All eyes turned eastward towards the hill in the distance. Shimon had already made up his mind and took a few moments to view it with a practiced eye, this site of the new home for his people.

Klud seemed to be able to read his thoughts.

“My Chieftain see's things no one else can." he said proudly.” His thoughts and words are often strange and unexpected, but his truth is always there."

Shimon turned towards the tattooed man with the dark slash of eyebrows and the badly broken nose. Normally he would have looked down on a mere warrior, from his lofty position as Chieftain, but he felt unexplainably humbled by his encounter with Parrish and the presence and power of the tall man and it just seemed right now to talk to Klud man to man.

"Has it always been so?"

“Yes. His actions can be beyond understanding but they always have a purpose. He can do strange things, mysterious things. I have seen him save and destroy both people and property. But he always wishes to do what is right and best. And not just for us of Dane-bre. For anyone that he can."

“It is true then, as I have heard, that he really is close to the Earth Goddess." Shimon's words were more of a statement than a question.

Klud just nodded proudly.

Shimon looked out once more across the green landscape before him, inhaled deeply the sweet, clean air and cocked his head to one side.

“It might not be such a bad thing then to live in the shadow of Dannu's man." he said softly.

“Not in his shadow." corrected Klud. "Under his care."

"Yes." Shimon nodded and smiled for the first time. Smiled at the warrior of another village. Someone who would normally be an enemy but with whom he now shared a sudden affinity. "I will abide by the rules laid down by your Chieftain and live on the east side of the river. It will not be so hard to keep this boundary of Parrish’s between us.”

He understood well enough how the benefits would vastly outweigh the problems. Besides, the river was by no means an un-crossable barrier. He felt sure exchanges would be made between groups, with or without his permission. He was after all Chieftain, understood those in his charge and knew that people would be people, no matter what restrictions were put on them. This boundary of Parrish's was in reality the simplest of partitions, put there by the tall man for the benefit of all.

"I will not tell Parrish of your decision." said Klud in a rare moment of diplomacy. "That honour is your alone, Chieftain Shimon."

"Thank you." Shimon bowed to Klud in respect, an unexpected gesture that surprised the warrior, although he took it gracefully enough.

Then the little band left the Danebury man to ponder on what might lay ahead. He watched as they set off down the slope towards the collection of wicki-ups along the tree line that housed Shimon's people. But not for much longer.

Tomorrow, after they had been visited by the great Chieftain of Dane-bre, they would break camp and move across this 'Parrish boundary' to their new home under the watchful, caring eye of Dannu's man.